## 思想者丛书
### （中英双语版）

SCIENCE
&
HUMANITIES

U0133096

# 密 尔 与
# 论 自 由

Mill's *On Liberty*

著 [英]George Myerson

译 王 静

**大连理工大学出版社**
DALIAN UNIVERSITY OF TECHNOLOGY PRESS

Mill's *On Liberty* – A Beginner's Guide.
By George Myerson
Copyright ©2001 George Myerson. All rights reserved.
ISBN 0-340-80473-4
©大连理工大学出版社 2008
著作权合同登记 06-2008 年第 111 号

**图书在版编目(CIP)数据**

密尔与《论自由》:汉英对照/(英)迈尔森著;王
静译.—大连:大连理工大学出版社,2008.10
(思想者丛书)
书名原文:Mill's On Liberty
ISBN 978-7-5611-4484-8

I.密… II.①迈…②王… III.①密尔,J.—人物研究—
汉、英②自由—研究—汉、英 IV.B561.49 D081

中国版本图书馆 CIP 数据核字(2008)第 146444 号

大连理工大学出版社出版
地址:大连市软件园路 80 号 邮政编码:116023
发行:0411-84708842 邮购:0411-84703636 传真:0411-84701466
E-mail:dutp@dutp.cn URL:http://www.dutp.cn
大连金华光彩色印刷有限公司印刷 大连理工大学出版社发行

幅面尺寸:147mm×210mm 印张:7.375 字数:140 千字
2008 年 10 月第 1 版 2008 年 10 月第 1 次印刷

责任编辑:梁 锋 张 敏 责任校对:知 轩
封面设计:宋 蕾

ISBN 978-7-5611-4484-8 定价:20.00 元

# 总　序

　　《思想者丛书》是一套有着深邃的科学与人文思想的丛书。丛书中既有伟大人物的介绍,也有对经典著作的解读。涉及杰出哲学家、科学家、艺术家及文学家的生平事迹,他们的时代背景、重大成就,特别是他们的思想(作品)的形成和发展过程,以及他们对其所处时代与人类文明进程的影响。这套丛书作为入门向导( A Beginner's Guide),能够把每一位伟大人物在学术或艺术上的突出贡献,以及在其著作中所阐述的深奥哲理,用极其通俗的语言加以简明扼要的阐述,并且时有画龙点睛式的提示,使一般非专业读者、特别是青年读者能够全面了解这些大思想家的突出贡献及其在历史上的作用和影响。

　　尤其值得一提的是,读者在阅读过程中可以了解他们的奋斗阅历、成功经验、切身体会以及对事业、对人生的执著追求,因而可以得到更多的启发,吸取更多的科学精神和人文精神的养料。对青年读者来说,会起到励志的作用,使得今后在自己的成长过程中,会时时感到这些潜移默化的影响;而对中老年读者来说,也可以对比自己的事业和人生经历,获得新的感悟。

这套丛书原文用英语撰写,目前在中国出版双语版。中文有较好的可读性,英文的文笔简洁明快。出版者保留了全部英文,可使读者在参照阅读的过程中体会不同文化的内涵。

大连理工大学出版社为了弘扬科学精神和人文精神,编辑出版了这套丛书,在我国出版业的百花丛中又绽放出一枝奇葩,实在是件值得高兴的事。

中国工程院院士

王众托

2008 年 6 月

# 出 版 者 的 话

对一个民族而言，
缺失人文的科学是麻木的，
缺失科学的人文是软弱的，
双重缺失则是愚昧的。

——任定成

1959 年，具有作家和科学家双重身份的英国著名学者C·P. 斯诺在剑桥大学作的一系列讲演中，提出了现代文化中普遍存在的困境：科学文化与人文文化的相互隔阂、互不理解。这后来成为一个具有世界影响的重大话题。事实上，在刚刚过去的 20 世纪，已经发生了的席卷整个世界的三次学术大战都是科学与人文之战，其中，斯诺的《两种文化》观点是第二次学术大战的导火索。

对于一名出版者而言，我们肩负着传承人类文明的重大责任，我们无力，也不可能成为学术之争的主角，我们所能做的，一方面是为思想"角斗士"们提供战场，幸运的是，这些战争的后果不是人类文明的浩劫，而是人类思想的繁荣；另一方面，我们有义务传播这些伟大思想，不仅仅是希望能够促进这两种文化之间更好地沟通，进而实现某种程度的理解和不同形式的整合，更重要的是希望更多的人能够在这两种文化的不断碰撞、不断融合中受益。为此，我们在努力着。

此次隆重推出的《思想者丛书》，就是我们系列出版计划的重要组成部分。

《思想者丛书》英文版由英国著名的 Hodder & Stoughton 出版公司出版，原丛书名为《A Beginner's Guide》。本套丛书涉及的领域非常广泛，从人物的角度来说，包括科学家、哲学家、艺术家、文学家等；从学科分类的角度来说，涵盖了自然科学、哲学、神学、心理学、政治学等。既有各位大师的生平、时代背景、思想及其影响介绍，也有其伟大著作的深度解读。这些人物和著作都具备如下特征：

（1）对人类文明的进程或对某一领域的发展起到重大推动作用；

（2）引发了有关思想及信仰的伟大运动，代表了该运动的精髓；

（3）具有高超的学术风格、才智及说服力。

鉴于此，本套丛书所涉及的均是影响世界的思想大师或读者渴望阅读的经典著作，即便在如今的互联网时代，这些人物及其作品仍散发着经久不息的魅力。现在，诸如短信、电子邮件等互联网时代的沟通方式极大地方便了人们的交流，但同时也使很多人的思想像夜空中的流星一样转瞬即逝。我们需要更能经得住时间考验的东西。这就是超越了时代，能够让我们以古鉴今、展望未来的思想大师及其经典著作。

　　但是,伟大的思想和作品却并不总是很容易让人领悟。尽管它们直接地呈现在我们面前,但其反映的是最为复杂的人类体验和观念。而本套丛书旨在将读者领进这些伟大人物或经典著作所描绘的世界并将其与自己的切身体验联系起来。为了使读者能够轻松愉快地阅读本套丛书,并能够比较容易地读懂这些思想大师的思想,每本书都大致按照以下写作思路编写:

　　(1)介绍大师们生活的时代背景、主要思想,相关重大事件及其对人类文明进程的影响;

　　(2)介绍思想大师的代表作,以及该作品的创作缘由及其影响;

　　(3)以审慎生动的方式来研习该作品的言论;

　　(4)解释关键术语及概念;

　　(5)援引简洁易懂的实例;

　　(6)提供深入探讨的问题。

　　本套丛书中的每一种都具有很强的连贯性,会使读者们孜孜不倦地从头看到尾——也许有些读者甚至会迫不及待地一口气将其读完。

　　时代的飞速发展更加引发了人们对精神家园的向往。让我们一起回顾伟大人物的时代,重温伟大思想的轨迹,共同感悟人类文明的进程。

大连理工大学出版社
科技教育出版中心
2008 年 6 月

# 目　录

## 密尔与《论自由》

# Mill's *On Liberty*

# 密尔与《论自由》

## Mill's On Liberty

# 引子：今天解读《论自由》

## 密尔——最合理的极端主义

### "当然没有人能反对……?"

思考一下这些强硬的道德教条：什么行为是完全正确或完全错误的呢？举出一个好人的例子或一条最邪恶的政策，然后试着与你自己进行辩论。你的道德信仰出什么问题了？用什么话可以驳倒"他是一个好人"的观点？你又是怎样为那条邪恶的政策来辩护的呢？

按照英国维多利亚时期自由主义哲学家约翰·斯图尔特·密尔的观点，如果你不能提出强有力的论据来反驳，那么你就没有充分理解你自己的信条。下面就是一条出自

《论自由》中的经典的陈述,为思想、言论和行为自由辩护的重要格言:

> 一个人对于一件事情若仅仅了解他所看到的那一面,那么他对这个事情就所知甚少。

III　　如果你还不知道对方——一个有着充分的论点和论据的反对者——将要说什么来驳倒你的观点的话,那么你就没有真正理解你为什么会持有这种观点。通常情况下,我们假设知道我们持有该观点的原因,当被要求解释该原因时,我们快速地找出正面的观点为之辩护。但密尔认为,我们并没有真正从根本上去了解我们所持有的观点和看法——除非我们也能看到相反的一面。强烈的信念是如此精确以至于我们很难找出它的相反面。

IV　　密尔的观点强硬,他的言论极具鼓动性。如果一个人不能提出合理的观点来反驳他所宣扬的价值教条的话,他就不应该持有此教条:

> 他的理由也许很好,并且没有人会驳倒他。但是假如他也同样不能驳倒反对者的理由,也不尽知那些理由都是什么,那么他便没有根据在这两种意见之中有所择取。

密尔一步一步地深入探讨。这部著作叙述详尽,理由    V
充分。但是,他也是一位极端主义者。《论自由》是合理的
极端主义的代表作:

> **密尔的合理的极端主义:辩论的方式**
> 如果辩论可以继续就不要中途停止。

在这一段中,密尔认为如果一个人不能看清事物的两    VI
面性,"他就没有理由"从中做出取舍。这里的"没有"是完
全没有,起强调作用。正是基于这一点,《论自由》中提到的
自由主义原则成为哲学史上和政治理论中最富感染力的观
点。每件事都有两面性或多面性,如果你只知其一,那么你
的观点就是片面、专制的,你就会随意地选择你的信条。你
的信条经得起问难吗? 你能保证?

**他们怎么能那样呢?**

想象一下世界上最可恶的人,与他们相关的一切事物    VII
都是令人厌恶的,你鄙视他们的每一种观点,讨厌他们的生
活方式。当他们说话时,他们提出的观点在你看来是卑劣
的,他们的语言使你发现的任何有价值的事物变得没有价
值。你厌恶他们的存在。根据密尔的观点,你的厌恶都是
你自己造成的。如果你愿意同他们交谈,你可以劝说那些
人改变他们的行为方式。但仅此而已,你并不能因为自己
的厌恶和愤怒而改变他们的行为方式:

有很多人把他们所厌恶的行为看作对自己的一种伤害而愤恨它,认为它对于他们的情感是一种暴行。

VIII 　　除了可以劝说那些讨厌的人之外,你并不能反对或禁止他们的生活方式。但是,密尔认为社会上一些带有限制性的条件和规则代表了这种思想:人们认为社会应当保护他们,抵制这种他们所厌恶的生活方式的存在:

公众在干涉私人行为时很少想到别的什么,只不过想到凡不同于他自己的做法或想法是怎样罪大恶极罢了。

IX 　　密尔认为每个人都是绝对自由的,所以别人可以冒犯我们,可以过我们极度厌恶的生活。这本书写于 1859 年维多利亚女王统治大英帝国时期,其中提出的观点始终受到人们争议,即使再过去 3 个世纪,人们仍然会继续争论。

X 　　我们所崇尚的价值观,应该允许人们去抨击和推翻!我们应该允许其他人过他们想过的生活,做出他们自己的选择。我们为什么需要其他人,不管他们是反对者还是谩骂者,不管他们能不能适应社会环境,他们是不是和我们观点一致,又或者其他什么?密尔的《论自由》都尝试着对这些问题做出解释。

## 密尔的自由主义观

### 无任何坏处就应平心静气

自由主义观存在于许许多多不同的事物:一场政治运 XI
动,一个理论,一系列的价值观,一种生活方式等。社会中
也有许多自由的思想家,他们总是提出反对意见,这也许正
是他们自由的原因!但任何自由主义者的核心都是自由。
自由的政治就是政治自由。伦理自由就是自始至终贯彻自
由的伦理。

《论自由》是自由主义的伟大著作,因为它对我们先前 XII
提到的论题,即个人与社会之间的辩论进行了讨论。和所
有自由主义者一样,密尔同样面临着这样一个问题:自由必
须有限度吗?根据密尔的观点,抵制一种生活方式或禁止
一种观点只有一个原因,即:

……能够施用一种权力以反其意志而不失
为正当,唯一的目的只是要防止对他人的危害。

如果一种行为没有伤害他人,人们就不能运用法律来 XIII
阻止它,这就引出了许多问题,我们稍后会讨论。但其中一
点是很明显的:你所谓的愤怒并不意味着真正的伤害。根
据自由主义者的观点,人们不能仅仅因为厌恶某些人或某
种生活方式就宣称受到伤害。相反的,正如我们所见,密尔

认为,令人不快的生活和不同的观点是必不可少的:他们对你有好处。社会与合理的极端主义者的争论,需要持不同观点的人们的责难。正因如此,《论自由》将自由主义者的思想推到了最前列。

XIV 　密尔从自由主义的观点出发,认为只有一个标准可以限定是否"伤害他人"。这必然引起争论。但有一件事是很明显的,伤害你的感情或破坏你的思想,这些都不能称之为伤害。他也举出了许多这方面的例子:

真的是伤害吗?

　　譬如有个意见说粮商是使穷人遭受饥饿的人,或者说私有财产是一种掠夺,那么这种意见如果仅仅是通过出版物在流传,那是不应遭到妨害的,但如果是对着一大群麕聚在粮商门前的愤激的群众以口头方式宣讲或者以标语方式宣传,那就可加以惩罚而不失为正当。

　　没有一个人应当单为喝醉了酒而受惩罚,但是一个士兵或一名警察则应当因为在执行任务时喝醉了酒而受惩罚。

XV 　总的来说,以下这些例子都体现了密尔的自由主义观。

XVI 　第一个例子讲的是表达上的自由。1859 年,那些"值得尊重的"公民们不同意人们自由地发表文章来谴责拥有个人财产这种行为,仿佛个人财产是他们偷来的一样。而密尔认为,除非在特定的环境下,即说那些话能产生直接的影响,否则谴责是没有坏处的。

> **密尔的自由主义意识：表达上的自由**
>
> 　　对于社会来说，没有什么价值或制度重要到需要社会保护来避免受到谴责和批评。

　　如果有人想写篇文章来表达对家庭、教育或警方的不 XVII
满，我们应该让他们写。事实上，或许当我们发现他们的观
点让人不满意时，我们越应该鼓励他们写。难道我们没有
信心为我们自己辩护吗？

　　第二个例子是关于角色和生活方式的。当今社会，英国 XVIII
立法机关提出不允许"精神错乱"的人上街。密尔则不会同
意这种做法，除非有人的确因此受到伤害。

> **密尔的自由主义意识：个人自由**
>
> 　　每个人的恶习与他人无关，除非有人因此受到直接伤害。

　　另外一个例子，维多利亚时期人们很讨厌酗酒，在著名 XIX
的禁酒运动时期的文章中也有所记录，但从密尔书中，我们
只看到当时政治家讨论的"小流氓文化"，即一群年轻人在街
上闲逛！密尔认为，社会没有正当的理由禁止任何人酗酒，
除非他承担某种社会工作，如飞行员等。

## 为什么今天阅读《论自由》？

### 与众不同的理由

　　我们经常认为思维是一个枯燥无味的过程，我们把"理 XX

性思考的"过程说成是"让自己镇定下来"的过程。处理某件事时,一个通情达理的人会采取中立吗? 会让步吗? 又或者什么都漠不关心? 通过阅读《论自由》,你会重新理解"什么才是合理的"。密尔的书充满了热情的合理性,合理的极端主义。

### 自由主义观

XXI　　目前,对《论自由》的辩论仍然很激烈。有些词仍然引人关注,它们意图劝我们承认我们还没有了解自由社会的根基是什么,还没有摆脱"奴性的趋同"达到个人的解放。密尔这位维多利亚时期的思想家仍然训斥我们不能认真地、按照惯例接受他人的观点和生活。我们真正了解在自由的社会生活意味着什么了吗? 在那里,每个人都有不同的信条,不同的生活方式。然而,我们还没有理解密尔的观点。

### 文化历史

XXII　　在读《论自由》时,我们可以查阅《话语的历史》及其关键词。密尔的著作在促进自由使用现代语言的过程中起到了很重要的作用。他的关键术语包括了我们在关于自由的争辩时仍然使用的词语:"多样性"、"个性化"、"一致性"、"干涉"等。他也对"公众意见"、"潮流"等主要概念做出了解释。

## 导读大纲

XXIII　　第一章　研究密尔的一生。主要根据其《自传》所写内容,并简要介绍他的时代背景。

第二章　讨论基本理论——自由。在《论自由》中解释　XXIV
了什么是自由的核心以及密尔的自由主义及其与功利主义
哲学思想之间的关系(《论自由》,引论)。

第三章　解释了密尔基本观点的另一面。他讲述了自　XXV
由与权威之间斗争的历史。尽管密尔因他的自由原则而闻
名,他却经常将理论与历史联系起来。实际上,密尔的历史
观点与他的自由论是一致的(《论自由》,引论)。

第四章和第五章　就密尔在《论"讨论自由和思想自　XXVI
由"》中提出的论点进行了阐释。首先,他对有关出版自由的
一些约定俗成的观点进行了分析,并列举了同时期的一个例
子:英国信息自由法案。其次,密尔系统地抨击了关于限制
表达自由的以往的一些观点(《论自由》,第二章)。

第六章　密尔积极为个人主义辩护,并提出了人民幸福　XXVII
的理论。其中引用了很多名言警句,陈述生动简洁,阐明了
密尔的论点(《论自由》,第三章)。

第七章　讲述了密尔眼中所处的社会,而他的社会批评　XXVIII
时至今日仍然有很大的影响。(《论自由》,第三章结尾的"个
人主义",第四章的"个人与社会",第五章的"应用")。

一

# 密尔的生活故事

1    约翰·斯图尔特·密尔在他的《自传》一书中讲述了一
个典型的生活故事,成为后来作家描述个人生活坎坷起伏的
典范。杰出的哲学家以赛亚·伯林把这本书称为"人类生活
最感人的描述之一"。本章中,我们将跟随密尔的生活故事,
并将其放在文中讲述。而这则故事直接关系到《论自由》的
中心思想。在这两本著作中,密尔把个性看做是人们幸福的
源泉。这个故事不仅仅是《论自由》的背景知识,更是其中的
一部分。

## 早年生活

约翰·斯图尔特·密尔 1806 年 5 月 20 日生于伦敦。他    2
的父亲是当时非常有影响力的思想家詹姆斯·密尔。在密
尔《自传》一书中，有一个非常有名的片段，是他对童年生活
的描述，当然，是一个哲学家的童年生活。尽管这本书的译
本有很多，但包括密尔在内，所有的人都认为他有一个与众
不同的童年，这也对他日后成为一个思想家有很大影响。很
重要的一点是，密尔给我们讲述了他父亲是如何教育他的，
从很小的时候在家中受教育直到 18 岁他到父亲的办公室上
班。约翰·斯图尔特·密尔从来没上过中学或大学，都是在
父亲独特的教育方式下学习。3 岁时他就学习了古希腊语和
算术。不久他被父亲带到田野上散步，并且背诵白天他所阅
读文章：

我阅读的时候做了许多笔记，早上散步时，我给他讲故事；我    3
读了很多书，大部分都是有关历史的：罗伯逊、休姆、吉本的
历史方面的书。

不久，密尔开始阅读米勒的《英国政府的历史视野》……    4
摩尔威的《教会历史》，麦克里的《诺克斯传》。

8 岁时，密尔开始学习拉丁语。他的这段生活故事即是    5
一长串关于各种不同语言的书籍的清单。童年时期阅读的
这些书籍对后期《论自由》的完成有直接影响，尤其是柏拉

图、亚里士多德、西塞罗等所写的关于政治理论的古代著作。从 12 岁起密尔开始学习逻辑学,也正因为此,长大之后,他成了这方面的权威。他孜孜不倦地阅读他父亲的著作《英国印第安历史》,这本书于 1818 年出版。密尔用赞叹的眼光重新回顾了这部著作:

　　这本书充满了日后被视为极端的民主的激进主义的想法与判断。

6　　　人们十分关注密尔在教育上缺失的那部分,尤其是宗教部分的缺失,为此密尔也很庆幸。从另一方面讲,正是由于这一方面的严重缺失,他的作品中缺乏感情。对于许多读者来说,特别是密尔的朋友凯雷,"这简直是噩梦般的童年"。而对于其他一些人,就像当时的哲学家乔纳森·莱里,他的评价就有点复杂,就像他是密尔一样。而父亲政治观点也持续影响着他的写作,在《论自由》中都有所体现。但以赛亚·伯林从另一角度出发,他认为我们可以把这本书看成是密尔反抗其成长方式的一种途径——强调个人的幸福生活,即人们应该寻找自己的生活和思考方式。

## 个人危机

7　　　密尔的父亲在东印度公司任职,当时这家公司负责印度的行政管理。1823 年,他介绍密尔在此任职,长达 35 年,期间他不断升职,位居高位,直至英国政府开始统治印度。

19世纪20年代早期，密尔积极投身于当时的政治和文   8
化圈。1822年至1823年冬，他创建了一个辩论协会，致力于
宣讲功利主义思想，这一哲理受到他父亲及与他们家世交的
边沁的赞扬。我们认为"功利"即是《论自由》讨论的主要内
容。边沁也做出了对"功利主义"的经典描述：

> 把功利原则描述成一种行为更合适一些……是   9
> 指人们一切行为的准则取决于是增进幸福或减少幸
> 福的倾向。

《道德和立法原则导论》

对功利主义最为经典的描述是"大多数人的最大幸   10
福"，这句话最早是由18世纪约瑟夫·普利斯特列提出的，
由边沁继承并发展。这些思想促进了功利主义以后的发
展，而密尔也以一种难以捉摸的批判的方式终身致力发展
功利主义。1823年，密尔创办了哲学激进主义期刊《威斯
敏斯特评论报》，在1824到1825年间，他忙于编写边沁的
法律著作。在1825到1830年间，密尔成为功利主义的代
言人。

与此同时，密尔痛苦地回忆了自1826年以来他所经历   11
的人生危机。在《自传》中他如实详尽地描述了这场变故，
也正因如此，《自传》不仅仅是哲学理论的参考内容，它也成
为了一部文学经典。这是一个令人吃惊的故事，讲述了关
于一个人精神崩溃及其长时间恢复的现代故事。

12　　　这则故事对我们从不同的方面理解《论自由》有直接帮助。密尔开篇便说：1826年秋，他一直精神萎靡，不久之后，无法克制的空虚感让他觉得生活毫无目的和价值，在这种枯燥沉重抑郁的心情下，他感到很孤独，尤其不能向独裁的父亲倾诉，而康复的过程更像是一场思想革命。在这则故事中，密尔讲他越来越清楚地认识到"人们幸福的必要性"。我们可以看到《论自由》的中心思想即幸福，这也是密尔一直宣讲的主题。此外，受华兹华斯诗学的影响，密尔第一次认识到"个人内在文化的价值。"

13　　　自1829年后，密尔退出了辩论协会。他声称脱离旧的"政治哲学体系"取而代之的是"复杂和多面的真正体系"。这种观点在《论自由》中也有所体现，其中它的内容和研究方法都是多样的。他的观点也影响了更多的人，其中包括莱雷，不管是个人生活还是作为一个作家都有很深的影响，还有柯勒律治以及德国哲学等。密尔也是法国革命的积极拥护者，但他不赞同他父亲盲目拥护的观点："民主是用于解决所有问题"的观点。

14　　　1830年，密尔遇到了他终生的挚爱哈丽特·泰勒，但由于哈丽特是有夫之妇且育有子女，此时他们只能成为密友。在她的丈夫去世两年后的1851年，两人才结婚。但在伟大的著作《论自由》即将完成和出版前，泰勒却死于肺结核，因此密尔用这本书来纪念她。事实上，为了赞许泰勒，密尔的这部著作及许多其他著作都是二人联名出版的。

## 作　品

约翰·斯图亚特·密尔出版过很多作品。他为不同的　15
刊物写了大量的文章。同时,他也出版了许多著作,在当时
产生了极大的影响。时至今日,仍然影响深远。

著作:

○ 1843 年春,他出版了划时代的著作《逻辑系统》,强　16
调知识来源于经验。这本书仍旧是现代逻辑发展的
主要教科书。

○ 1848 年,他出版了《政治经济学原理》,一经问世立
即对经济观点产生很大影响。

○ 1854 年,他编写了简本的《论自由》,1855 年《论自
由》书正式出版。

在《自传》中,他强调这部著作是与泰勒联名编著的。　17
在他看来,"《论自由》往往比我写的其他作品影响力更为
长久"。他把这本书看作是"一本关于一条真理的哲学教
科书",它的出版也宣布了"性格多样性和个性自由发展在
不同方面对社会和人类都很重要。"

在密尔看来,《论自由》也有不好的一面。他认为在将　18
来社会里,个性发展将会受到压迫,"在那个时候,《论自由》
中的教条才会发挥最大的作用。"

19 　　这是关于未来的哲学理论。1859 年,这本书一经出版便轰动一时,同年还出版了达尔文的《物种起源》。同时代的人对密尔的观点——尤其是他对所处时代的批评,持敌对态度。而人们对密尔的突然关注也标志着社会进入了一个新的时代,密尔成为主流思想的代表人物。1865 年,他成为一名国会议员,致力于增加妇女选举权,在此期间,他仍然写作。1873 年出版了伟大著作《自传》,同年去世。

# 二

# 理论上的自由

接下来的两章中我们将首次阐释密尔在《论自由》引论　20
中提出的基本观点。引论主要有两方面的作用,首先他把
自己的意识构筑成理论,其次,从历史观的角度来探讨问
题。在本章中,我们将分析《论自由》的理论基础。下一章
讲述密尔如何看待自由的发展史。

## 理论的序言:阐释"自由"

密尔用自己的观点来解释"自由":　21

公民自由或社会自由:探讨社会能合法施用于个体的权力的性质和限度。

摘录分析:

22

○ "公民或社会":密尔并没有讨论上帝统治下的人类自由意志,即自由和命运。他所谓的自由是指人类以群居或社会形式存的一种方式。他并没有谈及政治自由,理由接下来我们会讲到。

○ "权力":密尔经常从反面考虑问题。为了解释"自由"他引入了"权力"这一概念。自由被定义为权力实施的限度。

○ "合理":从文章开始,我们的论点便是价值的判定。密尔希望我们把社会看作是一个整体。对他来说,合理的社会可以解释为自由。如果一个社会逾越自由的限度实施权威,那么这个社会就会在我们稍后提到的自由合理性试验中失败。这可以说是密尔最有影响的成果。

○ "社会"和"个人":正如自由和权威一样,社会和个人是另一对反义词。个人自由的适用范围指的是社会干预的限度。

23

在这个摘录中,密尔是从对立面思考的。密尔采用特殊的方法从相反的方向理解每个概念的含义,这种叫做两极法。他采用动态分析法,并没有给出明确的定义:比如这就是社会或这就是个人。相反的,他更在意在不断变化过程中,一种观念对另一种观念的影响。如果我们从这个角度来观察社会,那么这种观念又对我们的个人观产生怎样的影响呢? 换句话说,他采用的是辩证法,用发展的眼光从反面来思考。

在写完这篇文章后,密尔声明自由的问题是鲜有提及的问题。他指出他的目标就是言简意赅地表明自由。　　24

## 密尔的写作意图:

* 密尔从新的角度来阐释自由。他认为这个问题迄今还没有被广泛讨论。　　25

* 密尔认为语言很重要。他想用语言来阐明一些先前没有提到的问题。

* 他最大的目的是增强语言在道德和政治争辩中的作用。

根据密尔的观点,以前从来没有提到的这个问题——自由,在许多争辩中都存在。哲学的任务是清晰地将隐藏在公众冲突、争论下的问题解释清楚。这个目标极有可能得到大家的认同。　　26

哲学家们揭示出这个“问题”才是社会动荡的源泉。在　　27

这些潜在的问题明朗化之前,所有的问题都很难解决。

## 密尔的自由合理性试验

28    密尔不想把自由问题仅仅描述为智力练习。在重新陈述自由时,他又提出了一个新的标准,用来讨论个人与社会的关系。

29    自由主义经常被认为是空洞无物的,而它的开放性吸引了很多人,但却始终找不到一条清晰的主线。自由主义者被看作是无拘无束的相对论者,其任务是辨别不同观点之间的差异。有人认为人们的观点天生具有局限性,我们的生活并不是绝对的,它取决于你是谁,生活在哪里。密尔并不同意这一观点。我们应该以自己的视角来观察世界。当要评价一个社会时,密尔不是一个相对论者。此时,他根据自由主义的教条提出了一个测试社会合理性的标准试验。

30    密尔把自由解释为确定社会合理使用权力。接下来,我们将从整体上来评价政策和社会。

> **密尔的自由合理性试验**
>
> 任何一个不尊重个人自由的社会都是不合理的社会。如果它侵犯了个人正当的权力,社会就不能使用其权威。

31    这种合理性试验是很随意的,因为它主要讨论自由等

问题。例如,可选择的合理性试验,是基于平等原则的基础
上提出的,即尽可能地实现最大化的平等。

现在我们回顾一下密尔提出自由这一观点,并演变为
评价一个社会的基本原则的过程。解释自由时密尔把自由
与权威这个词联系起来,此后,密尔又提出一条原则来测试
社会是否干预社会生活,是否使用权威:

> 本文的目的是要力主一条极其简单的原
> 则,使凡属社会以强制和控制方法对付个人之
> 事,不论所用手段是法律惩罚方式下的物质力量或者是公众意
> 见下的道德压力,都要绝对以它为准绳。

摘录分析:

○ "原则":首先,文章的目的是提出一条原则。这就
   引出了另一个问题,通常意义上,什么才是原则呢?
   什么情况下一个想法或观点会成为一条原则呢? 在
   政治理论的发展史即密尔的论述中,这一话题成为
   最难也是最核心的问题。

在密尔看来,一条原则是一个命题,它提供给我们思
考特殊问题的一种方式。作为一条原则,这个命题
必须广泛地适用于各个方面。另一方面,这一原则
不可能解决所有问题。一条原则有它的适用范围。
正如约翰·格雷在他的《重读〈论自由〉》一书中所

述,原则并不等同于规则。密尔的作品之所以有很大影响是因为他提出要用已知原则来判定社会应该何时来合理地实施其权威,何时超过界限。这的确是一个很有影响的声明。但能成为原则的还是极少数的。社会上并没有许多相关原则。事实上,密尔认为目前我们社会还没有清楚地认识这些基本原则。

○ "一条极其简单的原则":原则就是一贯的思考方式。其目的在于说明"为什么思考许多问题只需基于一条原则。"

○ "强制和控制":这条原则适用于刑事处罚和公众意见的道德胁迫等,像詹姆·斯蒂芬等早期评论家,他们强烈反对这种道德压迫:毕竟,那是维多利亚时代!换句话说,密尔虽然对法律感兴趣,但他也十分注意社会大趋势。他想探求在什么情况下法律会起到干预作用,例如吸食毒品或诈骗等。同时,除社会应该终止对人们施加道德压力外,他也强调了其他方面。

密尔希望政治和公民社会始终相辅相成。他不同意用强烈的道德压力来代替法律制裁。他们是不一致的,我们应该区分对待。应该受到法律制裁的案件往往更难处理。密尔不同意用道德恐吓来代替法律。

接下来讲到密尔书中最重要的部分：　　　　34

这条原则就是：人类之所以有理有权可以
个别地或者集体地对其中任何分子的行动自由
进行干涉，唯一的目的只是自我防卫。这就是说，对于文明群
体中的任何一员，所以能够施用一种权力以反其意志而不失为
正当，唯一的目的只是要防止对他人的危害。

摘录分析：

- "自我防卫"：自我防卫原则有积极的一面，它比其　　35
  另一意义——预防伤害其他人——出现得早。要
  使这两点都有意义，你必须把"自我防御"中的"自
  我"放在整个社会中，而不是单个地看问题。这不是
  为"自我防御"辩护的理论。它是社会驾于个人行为
  限度的范围。

- "人类"：如果这真是一条原则，那么它是普遍适用
  的。正因如此，密尔的文章既使人鼓舞又令人费解。
  我们不适用于这样的标准。我们有许多信条，并且
  被广大人民所接受：人类不应该野蛮，善良比恐吓更
  好。但我们不明白密尔为什么把这些观点运用在这
  里。他认为这条原则可以适用于整个人类社会，贯
  穿于整个时空和整个历史。

- "文明群体"：这里有一个特例：文明社会下的任何
  人。这条原则虽然普遍适用，但仍有些地方不能起

作用,即社会所在。在密尔看来,那并未开化。密尔承认,在原始状态下比在文明社会有时更应该限制个人行为。联系一下上下文,你会发现有些设想是互相矛盾的。这本书是由驻印度行政管理人员于大英帝国繁荣时期完成的。无疑,密尔在对王室的态度是积极进步的,但从他的文章中可以很明显地看出文明开化的人与其他人是有很大区别的。后来也有许多评论家坚持这种观点,例如格雷,"对现代社会来说这太严格了"。

36　　　滥用权威会侵犯社会合理的限度。密尔自由理论的核心便是"危害标准"。如果你没有足够的事实说明一种行为危害到其他人,那你就不能用法律或社会压力来阻止该行为。

---

**密尔的自由合理性试验:危害的标准**

　　只有在一种条件下可以限制个人行为,即当其行为将会危害到其他人时。如果在限度内实施权威,那么社会就是一个立法机构,否则是非法的。

---

37　　　如果法案超出危害标准的限度,社会将威胁人身自由。这是出现的最大的问题。自 1859 年赫顿之后,批评家们一直在想 "什么才能称之为伤害呢"? 很明显,身体受伤是伤害。但你不能说社会只能保护其成员不受身体伤害。如诈骗伪造、抢劫、诡计、谎话等,还有其他一系列的危害。这就引出了另一问题:情感和心理伤害算什么呢? 伤害他人感

情算是危害吗？什么又能决定一个人的感情是否受到伤害呢？

靠法律还是靠嘴说说？这条原则能持续多久？似乎他 38
只告诉我们应该如何去设定限度，但却不能用它来裁定什么才是好的法律，也就是说，只能决定什么是正当的法律，什么是法律。

### 密尔的自由合理性试验：举例

毒品和狩猎二者完全不同，但同时又是备受争议的两 39
个话题，而且是我们现时代的话题。我们用密尔的观点——社会驾于个人权威的限度是什么——来分析每一个问题。就毒品而言，问题的关键在于社会如何去保护个人。而狩猎，主要是社会当中的一部分如何合理地作用于其他一方。

密尔并没有提出简单的一条解决争论的方法，但他的 40
理论却给解决这个问题的方法指明了方向。看一下下面举的关于两个人的例子：

杰克，一个 18 岁的学生，非常支持禁止猎狐的法令。 41
他认为这种行为侵犯了动物的权利，法律应该禁止这种暴行。然而吸食轻微的毒品却是可以的，因为如果禁止尝试大麻或想要有类似心醉神迷经历的话，他们也许会说这侵犯了他们个人的权利。那就是为什么人们可以喝威士忌，而使用麻药却不合法。

42 　　玛格丽特,一个 43 岁的母亲,在农村一家商店看门。她强烈地反对颁布法令禁止猎狐。她认为这些陌生人打扰了他们的生活。她也强烈反对颁布法令禁止使用毒品,她认为应该组织一些活动来加强法律监管力度。

43 　　密尔不希望我们偏执地看待这些问题,我们应该做到以下几方面:

　　\* 首先,明确基本问题:自由是社会驾于个人权威的限度。

　　\* 其次,把"原则"应用于有争议的问题。

44 　　杰克和玛格丽特,这两个人是互相矛盾的,对猎狐和毒品立法,是两件完全不相关的事。密尔对人们观点和判断力的性质提出了质疑,在他看来,我们的判断力毫无原则可言。我们有我们自己的信条和观点,但我们从不把我们的信条用于原则测试。我们思考得前后一致吗? 我们禁猎的法令与禁毒的法令一致吗? 我相信我们给出的答案也是毫无原则。没有原则的不仅仅是个人,有时候,政治也会这样。我们有时也会听说政治家们做事缺乏原则。通常是指他们接受帮助时非常谨慎。但密尔的文章表明所有的政治领域内不准存在原则。政治党派总是在没有完全明白"情况是否前后一致"的情况下就探讨个人问题。

## 超越自由?

密尔在陈述其理论基础时遇到了一个更大的问题。我　45
们还应该需要什么原则呢? 怎样把其他原则与自由原则联
系起来? 怎样把它们用于实践来决定权威使用是否合理?
除自由理论外,密尔在其他两方面还有研究。

### 合理的标准

首先,社会上有一个标准来确定自由的限度。我们以　46
前已经提到过这个问题,在这里,密尔提出了更加公正的
看法:

　　　　自由,作为一条原则来说,在人类还未达到
　　能够自由地和平等地讨论而获得改善的阶段以
　前的任何状态中,是无所适用的。

摘录分析:

○ "能够":实际上,在这里,密尔解释了什么是文明。　47
　一个文明的社会是指生活在那里的人们,人与人,人
　与社会之间,都建立了良好的关系。

○ "改善":密尔在这里使用这个词是很危险的。我们
　可以看出密尔反对"改变他人"的观点。但是这里指

的是文明的人在没有受到任何强迫的情况下,自由地改变自己。

○ "自由地和平等地讨论":在文明社会,个人可以对他人的劝说做出反应。这是一种独特的观点,它超出了自由的限度。

48    除危害原则外,密尔也提出了合理性原则。他在文章中指出早在自由合理法性试验之前他就已经提出了合理性原则。在进行测验之前,你就应该证明社会符合合理性标准。在社会文明开化的前期,所有干预个人行为的人或事都被认为是不合理的。这就说明了密尔研究的并不仅仅只是自由。他还研究许多其他的理论。

**终诉:功利主义**

49    密尔是最早提出现代自由主义的思想家之一。他的有关自由的原则和思想是相辅相成的。但是,上一章我们提到了他也属于19、20世纪哲学的一个重要分支——"功利主义"。密尔在编著《论自由》的同时,他也编写了另一部著作《功利主义》,揭示了功利主义在生活中的重要作用。

50    我们可以看出功利主义者思考的核心不是自由,而是功利。批评家们批评密尔没有指出功利与自由的关系。功利指的是一种行为、一个决定或一件事产生幸福或减少痛苦的能力。我们必须运用功利来做出很多决定。我们应该功利一点,即做事要把痛苦缩减到最小化,使快乐最大化。

这不仅适用于我,也适用于很多人,因此,这并不是单纯意义上的自私。在这之后,密尔便把功利与自由联系起来讨论:

> 的确,在一切道德问题上,我最后总是诉诸功利的;但是这里所谓功利必须是最广义的,必须是把人当作前进的存在,而且是以其永久利益为根据。

摘录分析:

○ "最后":当需要做决定时,我们优先选择功利。影响你做决定的主要是你做的判断是否基于产生幸福减少痛苦的基础上。　　　　　　　　　　　51

○ "永久利益":这个词十分重要。密尔没有讨论瞬间行为的影响或一个人获得的暂时性的快乐,而是其产生的永久结果、成本利益等。著名的思想家柏林曾经研究过如何理解利益。

○ "把人当作前进的存在":真正的功利主义是研究怎么才能使一个人快乐,什么才能帮助人们在不断的成长过程中获得幸福。

我们现在对密尔的研究方法有了大概的了解,最重要　52
的是我们知道他持有许多的观点。尽管本书只讨论了一个问题,即个人与社会的关系,但密尔并不是只坚持一种观点的思想家。

53    关于自由这个问题,讨论的中心是用危害原则进行自由合理性试验:没有伤害意味着没有达到限度。

54    但是,除了自由之外,密尔还需要研究其他两方面:

1.合理性原则:没有文明的思考就没有自由。

2.最后的诉求——功利:在很大程度上以获得人类幸福的最大利益进行选择。

55    密尔的真正问题是研究这些思想有何关联。这并不是一个个人问题,他是解释自由理论中出现重大问题的关键。这虽然用来解释个人自由是可以的,但对于解释什么是一个好的社会、什么是好的政策、如何运用权力等问题时就不充分了。

56    一些评论家认为,密尔并没有明确地回答怎样处理自由与合理性及功利性的关系。人们一般认为他是披着自由主义外衣的功利主义者。其他人则批评他为了进行论证这个论点混淆了许多概念。

57    密尔的辩解中提到了两点:

1.密尔是一个辩证的思想家。他并没有提出规则或体系,只是提出我们必须权衡二者关系。这个权衡的过程就是辩证的过程,即我们把不同势力置于相反的两面考虑。密尔旨在强调一个过程,而不是得出一个结论。

2.密尔提出的自由原则不是用来做选择或政策的测

试。这点很重要,因为这把密尔同其他思想家区别开来。没有人比密尔更认真地谈论自由。但是当时他并没有意识到他是第一个在文章中谈及自由主义的人。他对现代政治和文化产生了良好的作用。

三

# 历史上的自由

58    我们已经知道密尔是怎样提出自由理论的,以及该理论如何产生极大的影响。但事实上,密尔的自由主义观点还有另一方面的意义——历史意义。本章中,我们主要探求密尔对人类历史随着自由主义的演变而发展的研究。没有这段历史,理论就不会存在。密尔不是只会空想的思想家。他总是努力把原则与现实社会和真实历史联系起来研究。实际上,《论自由》研究的并不仅仅是关于历史的,也是关于价值的。

## 人类的进步

上一章我们学习了密尔的功利主义原则,即人类作为 59
不断进步的存在所获得的长久的利益。从密尔的历史进步
观点来看,历史是不断前进的人类表达自己思想的地方,但
并不是表达自满或单纯。

密尔和马克思都认为历史并不仅仅是指过去以及过去 60
发生的事,它还包括现在和将来。换句话说,历史是一个不
断发展的过程,包括很多年代:

……人类中比较文明的一部分现在已经是
进入的进步阶段了。

摘录分析:

○ "阶段":在这里,我们更愿意使用另一个名词,"历 61
   史时期"。这个词是中性的,它是随意的一个时间
   段。在密尔看来,"阶段"是一个展开的过程。马克
   思、黑格尔、康德都同意这种看法。

○ "文明的一部分":密尔讨论时紧紧围绕着人类社会
   的同一性。在他看来,尽管有些部分更文明,但它们
   始终都是一个整体。文明指的不是道德或技术的发
   展,而是指自由平等地讨论。在历史进程和人类发

展二者之间有一个相同点，它们都是从低级向高级
自然发展的过程。

○ "人类"：密尔的《论自由》出版于 1859 年，同年也出
版了达尔文的《物种起源》。人类历史中除了有逻辑
的形成过程，还包括自然历史的形式。

62　　维多利亚时期人们对进步的认识看起来似乎有些自
满。为什么有人认为历史会不断地前进。20 世纪的危机似
乎推翻了这种想法，但是，实际上，进步还表现在另外一方
面。为了避免人们满足现状，密尔使用了"进步"来向他所
处的时代挑战。"现在"只是一个简单的过程。有人认为维
多利亚时代是黑暗的，应该开创更美好的明天。

63　　历史的第一个特征就是进步，而第二个特征就是斗争：

自由与权威之间的斗争，是我们最早熟知
的历史中最引人注意的那部分。

摘录分析：

64　　○ "最早的"：历史从什么时候开始？戏剧的第一个剧
目是什么？在密尔看来，历史从斗争开始。毫无疑
问，在斗争前还有一个过程，但是它们从不包括在历
史之内。历史时期的变更是由于冲突的发生。历史
是处于根基地位的两个事物相互斗争的过程，社会

的存在是由于敌对的双方不断夺取政权。

○ "斗争"：19世纪流行的是黑格尔的历史哲学，其哲学的核心是"斗争"。在他看来敌对的双方在不同的思想下推动历史前进。

1. 马克思采用黑格尔的方法把历史看作是不断的斗争。

2. 研究历史用到的这个词语具有辩证性。

黑格尔认为，辩证就是两种思想间不断的斗争。马克思认为，辩证就是不同社会力量，即阶级之间的斗争。19世纪就是资产阶级和工人阶级不断斗争的时期。而密尔对辩证有自己的理解。辩证就是随着人类社会的不断发展揭示自由及其对立面的矛盾。

## 自由的辩证法

在上一章，我们知道密尔如何从普遍意义上解释自由　65
原则：自由是用来判定社会和个人两者之间关系是否合理的标准。但现在我们看到了他的另一观点。自由是指不同的事情反抗其对立面的一段历史。

> **密尔关于自由的辩证主义观点：**
> 人类历史体现了社会两种观念的斗争：个人和权威之间的竞争。

66      正如大家所了解的密尔研究的历史是,希腊,罗马和英国的历史。格林强调,密尔关于历史属于西方、起源于希腊的推断丝毫没有可以质疑的地方,还有一点奇怪的地方就是他把英国与罗马、希腊联系起来,与其说是现代社会的历史不如说是维多利亚时期的神话。而从另一方面看,密尔对历史的形成有独到的见解。

**第一阶段:专制时期**

67      在第一阶段,自由和专制是相对立的:

所谓自由,是指对于政治统治者的暴虐的防御。

68      密尔所谓的历史始于人民完全被压制的时期:

**密尔关于自由的辩证主义观点:**

第一阶段:最初的专制暴政阶段

专政统治阶段,自由是人们用来抵抗独裁统治的工具。

69      在第一阶段中,统治者认为他们可以为所欲为。在他们看来,人民不过是他们随意使用的工具。密尔把原始社会解释为独裁统治。政治最初是独裁的,没有自由而言。自由是这种政治体制的对立体。

> **定义 : 政治**
>
> 　政治最初只是一种纯粹的权力；而自由的开始只是政治势力的替代品。

　　在历史发展的第一阶段，即专制统治阶段，政治是表达　70
统治者意志的工具。一切事物都被排除在政治之外。这一
点很重要，因为自由此时不属于政治范畴，是其对立体。自
由与统治者的意志相反：

>
>
> 　　　　　统治者被看作是……对于其臣民来说必然
> 的对立者。

　　希腊的民主政策是一个特例：它标志着一个新事物的　71
到来。但总体上来说第一阶段意义清楚明了：统治者镇压
被统治者。

　　在第一阶段，自由作为一种社会观念出现，反对政治统　72
治。统治者发明了政治，被统治者创造了自由。因此密尔
没有把自由看成是一种政治原则而是社会原则，它与政治
权力截然相反。国家不是自由产生的源泉，而是它的敌人。
自由产生于政治之外。

> **定义 : 原始的自由**
>
> 　自由是由社会创造，用来抵抗政治力量。

73     自由这个观念是被统治的人民提出来用于反抗政治专制统治的。正是这种专制统治产生了自由。

74     从这一点上可以看出密尔所有的观点。自由的原意只是一个消极的观念——对专制统治的反抗。卢梭曾提出人生来是自由的:这被称为是浪漫的自由主义。密尔和马克思认为自由产生于对镇压的社会反抗。自由并不是个人原有的状态,相反的,自由产生于社会反抗统治者的独裁统治。这很重要,因为很多人批评密尔个人主义色彩太浓。从这里我们可以看出密尔认为自由是社会的产物。

### 第二阶段:民主的产生

75     历史上的每一个阶段都可以根据对自由的定义来划分。第一阶段,自由是政治统治者绝对统治的限度。当人民开始进入政治领域时,第二阶段开始了。此时,自由失去了本来的含义,新的斗争出现:

此斗争随着被统治者的定期选择而前进。

76     在这个阶段,统治者与被统治者之间已经没有斗争。相反的,人民提出了一个积极的目标:让统治者为他们服务。与此同时,民主社会产生,同时法国大革命爆发。

> **密尔关于自由的辩证主义观点:**
>
> 第二阶段:民主的产生
>
> 民主精神试图利用权力为社会服务。自由不再是被统治者反对统治者来保护自己的工具,而是权力需求的一部分。

　　自从人们渴望获得权力,他们不再把自由当作保护自 77
己的工具。相反,他们认为一旦他们获得权力,他们就会获
得自由。

> 国家无须对自己的意志有所防御。

摘录分析:

○ "国家":这是 19 世纪政治和历史上的一个重要概 78
念。民主的出现代表了国家的产生,这也被称作"国
家独立自主"。

○ "意志":19 世纪哲学史上对"意志"的解释有很多
种。卢梭在其民主理论的基础上提出了人民的"共
同意志"这一说法。

> **第二阶段:自由**
>
> 自由意味着获得权力,而不是防御权力。

　　当人民获得权力时,专制统治自然不可能存在。如果 79

社会本身就是暴君:"那就不怕对自己的专制统治了。"

80      在第一阶段,统治者和被统治者,政治和社会之间存在矛盾冲突。在第二阶段,被统治者试图变成统治者,而社会控制了政治。社会通过政治进行自我管理。在这种情况下,自由的本意已经减少。

81      这是密尔辩证地看待自由的最好的例子。社会发展经历了不同时期,自由的含义也的确发生了改变。自由的历史有两方面,一是一种思想随着历史的发展而发展——自由的思想。一是一种思想随着时代的演变不断地发生变化。

### 第三阶段:多数派的专制统治

82      从先前的两个阶段我们已经展望到了第三个阶段。在这个阶段中,统治者对人民的暴虐统治产生了一种新的形式——"多数的暴虐"。

83      第三阶段主要是自由的辩证发展过程。统治者对人民的统治产生了一种新的形式。当然,在密尔的时代民主还达不到这个程度——他个人支持扩大公民选举权,尤其是增加妇女选举权——但由于是大多数人的专制统治,所以在这里他指的并不仅仅是选举的作用:

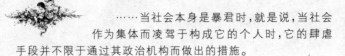

……当社会本身是暴君时，就是说，当社会作为集体而凌驾于构成它的个人时，它的肆虐手段并不限于通过其政治机构而做出的措施。

摘录分析：

○ "集体"：我们之前举过一个例子，人们错误地把"集体"看作是"个人"的反义词。在这篇文章中，我们看到社会和个体都是矛盾的。社会由个体组成，但这个集体过着相对独立的生活，并把自己看作是独立个体的对立体。 84

○ "政治机构"：这是一个对民主制度下选举出的领导人和代表们的讽刺术语。"官员"一词暗含了的资产阶级的性质。密尔在担任国会议员期间，曾提醒参选人，他们会被自己的意志束缚。

多数派的人都有一套实现自己意愿的方式。而政治不过是他们用来控制少数派的一种武器而已。在第三阶段，主要是专制统治的多数派与被压迫的少数派之间的斗争。 85

| 密尔关于自由的辩证主义观点 | 社会结构 | 权力结构 |
| --- | --- | --- |
| 第一阶段 | 原始社会 | 统治者对人民的绝对控制 |
| 第二阶段 | 民主运动 | 人民控制统治者 |
| 第三阶段 | 民主制度确立 | 多数派的专制统治 |

86　　　统治者与被统治者,暴君与人民之间的不断斗争过程中,民主应运而生。而此时斗争的双方变成了多数派和少数派或个人之间的斗争。一开始,社会就是政治权力所利用的工具,但现在社会也沦为被镇压的部分:"共同的社会",是共同意志与个人愿望之间的斗争,是以全体一致与个体差异之间的斗争。第三阶段也是社会压迫的时期。

87　　　很明显,密尔认为他所在的社会,虽然还不太完善,但已经进入到了第三个阶段。事实上,这是一个现代社会,或大众社会。现在,自由又意味着什么呢? 它不再与绝对统治者相对立,而是和多数派相对立:

> 集体意见对独立个人的合法干涉是有一个限度的。

---

**密尔关于自由的辩证主义观点:**

第三阶段:民主制度的确立

自由即多数派对少数派或个人专制统治的限度。

---

88　　　纵观历史,自由的含义颠倒了:这是一种辩证的思想。一开始,自由是指反抗专制统治者的暴力统治。而到了第三阶段,自由变成了反抗多数派的专制意志。自由的含义随着实施专制的对象性质的改变而改变。实际上,每个阶段,自由的定义都不相同,这就是密尔历史的辩证的观点。

密尔的自由主义理论属于第三个阶段,"多数派的专制　89
统治"。在他看来,这个阶段并不好。在前一阶段,专制统
治从外在可以体现:残酷的镇压,肉体的摧残。人们也可以
通过行动进行反抗。而现在,专制统治却改变了实施方法,
它转为对人们一致的镇压,"社会专制统治"比"政治镇压"
更凄惨,因为人们更难反抗:

······它给逃离留下很小的余地,更深地透
入生活的细节,甚至浸入灵魂。

这是《论自由》中提到的最黑暗的部分,让人极度地绝　90
望。而这部分也经常被忽略,他强调了自由主义哲学积极
的影响以及其判定的标准——危害标准。但此时密尔也看
到了不足的一面,他认为随着社会的进步,一种新的更为可
怕的镇压方式也会产生。

| 历史阶段 | 现代性:第三阶段 | 传统性:第一阶段 |
| --- | --- | --- |
| 镇压机构 | 社会多数派 | 政治独裁 |
| 镇压工具 | 外部力量 | 内在影响 |

根据密尔对历史的研究,第二阶段产生了民主,它是传　91
统社会与现代社会的一个过渡期。在现代社会,人民成了
压榨自己的工具。如同镇压少数派一样,多数派也残酷镇
压其内部成员。在现代社会,没有人是自由的。

### 关于第四阶段：一致还是分裂？

92        密尔的自由理论与多数派的镇压是相对应的。他的理论普遍适用，但在马克思看来，该理论在历史发展中也有重要作用。社会进步就会产生新的暴力统治，因此这些时代都是危险的。还会不断的有新的暴力统治出现：

 多数人还没有学会去体认政府的权力就是他们的权力，政府的意见就是他们的意见。

93        当多数派能灵活运用权力时，新的专制统治马上就会产生。任何异端行为都被看作是反动的。法律成为镇压异端人群的工具。

94        然而，多数派还没有真正了解他们的任务。人们仍然保留着前一阶段所持有的观点，即政府反对大多数人的意志。旧的自由仍然保留着许多古老的特征。但随着时间的推移，人们会逐渐认清他们的所处的环境，继续探求另一条关于个人自由的教义。在下一阶段，自由成了少数派维护自己的工具，成为多数派要铲除的对象。

> **密尔关于自由的辩证主义观点：**
>
> 关于第四阶段
>
> 将来，多数派会完全控制国家；自由成为他们要铲除的对象。
>
> 就少数派以及认清独立存在的个体而言，自由成为一条与众不同的原则。

与马克思不同，密尔不认为他的历史辩证主义观点给　95
未来指明了方向，但的的确确暗示了未来不同的发展方向。
很明显，这有不好的一面，在多数派的统治下权威当局履行
这一原则。

> **第四阶段的黑暗：**
>
> 同一性的时代

不管怎样，人们还是有希望的。辩证地看问题加剧了　96
危机，自由这个概念表现了激进的意义。面对普遍一致性，
反对者打出了自由这面旗帜：

>
> 唯一实称其名的自由，乃是按照我们自己的道路去追求我们自己的好处的自由。

总的来说，社会也有一段个人发展的时期。将来，自由　97
会变成社会的主要思想，多样性会取代一致性，成为社会

原则。

---

**第四阶段的光明：**
多样性的时代

---

98    新的时代还没有到来，但密尔的对历史的观点有点乌托邦的色彩。也许当人们真正可以自由地追求自己理想的时候，不论好坏，这场争斗才会结束。如果那样的话，辩证地讲，人类也许会从一致性的时代进入另一个新的时代——多样性的时代。

# 四

# 出版自由和公众兴趣自由

　　现在我们开始讨论密尔文章的关键部分,《论自由》中 99
的第二章"论思想自由和讨论自由"。在这一章中,它探讨
了言论自由,现代自由论中最基础的一部分,也是对密尔影
响最大的部分。密尔帮助制定了自由言论的议程,他的分
析常被用来解决当前社会的一些争端,如国家政府法律以
及某些个人机构等企图控制公众意见和言论。我们将从历
史的角度和相关视角来仔细研究密尔对公众表达自由的讨
论。我们着重讨论出版自由,因为这部分的议论非常精彩,
与本章中其他部分有直接关系。

## 步骤一:公认观点的确定

100 　　在"论思想自由和讨论自由"中,密尔一开始就提出人
们应该认识潜在的原则,这一观点是他在"出版自由"的基
础上提出的。大概,他的声明表面上看起来很有自信,但现
在已经没有人再去管什么是基本自由。人们认为应该出版
自由,但是这样的吗? 他所强调的这一部分真的是出版自
由想要表达的吗?

101 　　在这里,密尔给出了解释,但在这个过程中,我们知道
这个话题具有预见性,因为他的目标是去除关于这些重要
公众讨论中的熟悉的观点,不断促进新的观点产生。实际
上,密尔把历史辩证的观点运用到具体实例中。他是为了
说明"出版自由"这一观点产生于前一阶段的自由的历史辩
证观点。除非重新考虑新形式,这个有价值的想法将会是
破坏性的。

102 　　首先,他给出了出版自由原来的解释:"出版自由"是反
对腐败政府或暴虐政府的保证之一。在这一方面,它是指
限制一个不是建立在民主和公众控制下的政府。没有一个
在利害关系上与人民不一致的立法机关或行政机关可以硬
把意见指示给人民并且规定何种教义或何种论证才许人民
听到,这个理论也是从第一阶段得出的。

**步骤一：**

出版自由：公认的概念

一贯原则：如果一种权力或政府不能代表公众的话，那它就不能控制公众的思想。

在密尔看来对出版自由的这种理解是从他们前辈那里 103 传下来的。自由来源于一些历史事件，如 17 世纪的英国内战、国王及他们任命的管理者们对政治及宗教的迫害。这些事件促使第一阶段的自由主义结束。

这是密尔写作技巧的一个典型例子。它主要指出有些 104 话是怎样从他所处的年代传下来的。如果我们继续使用以前的语言——在没有其他语言适合我们的情况下——我们会重复以前的讨论。他已经为"自由"这个基本观点应用于公众讨论做好了准备。在目前的历史阶段，旧的自由已经过时了。出版界已经不用再反抗专制统治了。

我们将从"出版自由"中体现的传统意义开始研究，逐 105 步过渡到"论思想自由和讨论自由"中所体现的现代意义。这个概念来源于多数派专制统治时期——我们前一章讲到的第三阶段。现在，权力已从暴君手中传到了人民手中。旧的防卫式自由已经过时，新的威胁已经出现，在第三阶段，多数派的意志已成为主要威胁。

密尔很巧妙地引导读者理解了自由的意义。应该给予 106 出版自由，包括所有想要听取的意见——如果政府不是代表公众的意见,那他就不能干预这种自由。密尔慢慢地引导读者一步一步了解这个概念。但是,如果你停止讨论,你就不会在讨论中明白其中的逻辑关系。当政府更具代表性时,又会发生什么呢?密尔认为,出版自由的提出是用来防御不具代表性的政府、独裁的暴君以及其他专政统治者的。19世纪中期,产生了选举制。的确,当时选举范围还很小,密尔要求扩大选举权。但是维多利亚时期政府已经不是政府随意地使用他们权力的时代了。当政府逐渐代表广大人民的利益时,旧的自由原则又会变得怎样呢?

## 步骤二:公认观念的解构

107    密尔试图让我们思考什么才是出版自由。他保证或似乎保证——除非出现特别的恐慌情况下,政府不会压制公众舆论。除了即将到来的革命,19世纪思想启蒙的当局权威不会退后到过去的统治下。那是一种讽刺。接下来密尔讨论的是下一阶段的特征:

> **步骤二:**
>
> 传统意义的"出版自由":一种讽刺的观点
>
> 现代社会,政府在没有极端恐慌和法律受到威胁的情况下可以保证出版自由。

108    有时我们会想,如果政府在一些危急的情况下反对出版自由的话,那这种自由还有真实性可言吗?当公众舆论变得必不可少愈演愈烈时,这是一种危机吗?

　　此时,密尔讽刺得更激烈了。讨论进入到了第二阶段,　109
即"出版自由"固有意义的解构。密尔向我们揭示了这种看
似很好很明确的文字本身的矛盾性。他让我们看到了一些
自相矛盾的话,正是这些话使"出版自由"的古老教条彻底
瓦解。在现代社会,旧的"自由"被当作是一种工具,当权政
府可以大范围地频繁地进行审查。事实上,任何宣称自己
可以代表大众的权威当局,除了公众利益接受审查外,他们
允许人们思想绝对的自由。历史辩证法已经彻底地改变了
传统意义上的出版自由——他的作用不再是保护人民反对
暴君,而是反抗当局政府对人民的压制。

　　密尔看似平常的逻辑推导中也是出现经典之处。他向　110
我们保证,在立宪制国家中,即公民在一定程度上享有选举
权时,政府"不会约束人们表达思想自由"。似乎,在政治民
主和讨论自由之间有一定联系。这种联系也体现在出版自
由为公众利益服务上。

　　当然,密尔补充说政府不会仅仅因为自己的喜好和判　111
断就反对其他观点。没有一个政府如此自大。相反,立宪
制政府只有在确定出现如下情况时才会出面制止:

……一般公众不复宽容的机关。

摘录分析：

112　　○ "不复宽容"：容忍是自由哲学理论和实践上最早用
　　　　到的一个概念，它最先出现在反抗宗教迫害中，也
　　　　成为对待不同生活和价值观的通用方法。自由的
　　　　对立面过去是宗教迫害，而现在演变而来的是忍受
　　　　精神。这一点我们从与密尔同时代的属于自由主
　　　　义另一派的马修·阿诺德身上也可以看出。

　　　　○ "公众"："公众"这个概念产生于民主时期。公众是
　　　　一个集合精神。当要镇压少数派和异教徒时，多数
　　　　派就充当了公众的角色。公众即占多数派的，他拒
　　　　绝任何异端人士。

　　　　○ 换句话说，如果出版自由指的是有权表达任何观点，
　　　　且这种观点是公众所愿意听到的，那么，我们可以说
　　　　政府代表了大众，代表了他们的利益，因此他们有权
　　　　力或者有义务抑制大众不愿听到的观点。

113　　旧的自由教条还远远不能改变整个世界。曾经一段时
间内人们享有很大的自由，即公众有权去听他们想要听到
的言论。而那段时间指的是绝对的专制统治反对自由讨论
时期，他们根本没有考虑公众的意愿，只是习惯性地反对公
众利益。不管是正式还是非正式的，当政府开始在公众意
志下执政时，旧的自由就不能再保护自由的言论了。现在，
密尔试图对旧的自由观念和新的合理性试验进行比较——
用是否产生实际危害来判定政府干涉与否。

密尔预见了一个黑暗的未来：没有自由的民主。在民 114
主时代，甚至是半民主或四分之一民主的时代，我们需要一
种新的自由理论。旧的自由——为了人民的自由——只是
服务于当权机构。你能体会到现在我们所倡导的自由已不
是过去意义上的自由。密尔从解构主义角度证明了：一个
众所周知的词可以有另外一种理解方式。密尔给"自由"做
出了新的解释：解构之后的重构，《论自由》后半部分就是不
断地讨论这个过程——"限制多数派意志的自由重构"。

密尔告诉了我们为什么关于自由的传统教条不能保证 115
自由的民主性。出版自由可以保证人民讨论的自由，最大
限度地进行思想和言论交流，但是密尔指出随意地使用这
个词会产生反作用。出版自由有可能成为某些教条的基
石，如控制和限制人民的教条，也有可能成为民主化审查制
度的基本原则。如果人们仍然认为自由就是公众意见或利
益，或认为自由是立法政府所享有的权利的话，那么以上所
述的反作用都有可能发生。

**步骤二：**

传统意义上的"出版自由"：解构

没有政府可以限制公众讨论，除非：

* 政府可以完全代表公众讲话，或与公众利益一致时；
* 立法秩序受到极端威胁时。

实际上，此时我们陷入迷茫：密尔用充满讽刺的语言解 116

释已知术语,此举的目的是什么？在代表公众意见方面,政
府做得越好,在证明"限制多余思想这种行为"的正当性方
面,就会越差。用"出版自由"来阻止政府限制任何扰乱公
众的思想,其本身并没有什么。政府允许绝对自由,除非这
种高压政策损害人民利益或明确表明与大众呼声一致。旧
的自由主义成为新的暴君产生的基础。

---

**传统意义上的"出版自由"：不可能理解的悖论**

　　政府是代表大众的,反映大众心声的,他做得越好,越有
权力限制大众表达他们想要表达的观点和意见。

---

117　　同样的自由,在一个时代可能是革命性的,在另一时代
也许支持政府镇压。这种辩证的观点反映在密尔探讨批判
或解构阶段。这种观点远远超出他在文中所讨论的具体实
例和文本。

## 21 世纪对密尔的研究

118　　密尔为更全面地讨论言论自由和思想自由也做了充分
准备。很明显,他认为对自由应该有许多不同的解释,这一
点非常必要,这样政府和公众就很难压制那些不想听到的
思想和观点。但是,在我们讨论那些观点前我们应该考虑
一下与分析出版自由的教条相关的一些内容,并把它们与
当今政府与媒体的关系联系起来。在我们的时代,怎么进
行密尔的自由合理性试验呢？

仔细研究后你会认为,密尔的研究已经过时了,他所讨 119
论的内容都是 19 世纪中期的,我们应该认清《论自由》属于
他的时代,这一点是很重要的。密尔描述了民主的前景,而
我们生活在他之后的年代。密尔没有等到真正进行有意义
的选举的时代,社会和绝对霸权之间的斗争仍然记忆犹新。
但他的观点在某些方面仍然对我们有直接的影响。

## 21 世纪的民主审查制度

政府管理和限制公众舆论的主要方式是控制他们了解 120
信息。很明显,如果公众不能了解更多的信息,就不能参与
讨论。因此,最强有力的监控制度就是控制信息——我们
了解的大多数信息都是在政府的控制之下。政府这种控制
信息的权力即来源于民主管理。作为我们的代表,政府有
权替我们选择信息,如果不加选择,那将会对人民利益产生
极大危害。拿安全问题举例,如果消息泄露,有可能造成人
们不必要的恐慌,引起经济危机,当然,在这方面仍然存在
着争论。

另一个例子,"如果部长和政府官员出现意见分歧"这 121
个消息泄露,就会让恐怖分子和军事敌人有机可乘。

在英国,这个问题引发了公众对信息自由的持续讨论。 122
1914 年,保守党执政,政府实行开放政策——即信息能否获
取主要取决于"危害测试"。实际上,这与密尔的合理性试

验或危害标准相符合。但21世纪的今天政府和政治家们
实施这一原则有点过于强硬。

123　　人们仍然举行活动要求扩大信息量,但同时他们也支
持合法地、长久地进行"危害测试"。密尔认为限制自由唯
一的目的就是为了防止"伤害"——参与活动者认为,危害
并不都那么显而易见,所以公众有了解全部信息的权利。

124　　1998年,工党执政,新政府领导人首相布莱尔起草文
件,设立信息自由执行官,享有要求某个机构发布"公众关
心的问题"的相关信息权利——但并不是控制信息发布的
权利。

125　　内政大臣杰克·斯特罗见证了关于扩大信息接受和讨
论自由等法案的实施:

　　……法案要求权威考虑公布信息,对问题
作出详细的解释,包括公众兴趣。

126　　批评家尖酸刻薄地讽刺说:"内政大臣有权决定是否是
出于公众兴趣而发布信息"。这是关键问题。谁来决定"什
么才是公众感兴趣的呢?"政府认为他们必须对信息发布负
责,这就引出了另一个讨论:"信息决定权掌握在信息大臣
手中这未免'太不民主'"。

127　　这场争论与密尔在1859年讨论时所设想的一样。政

府是民主选举产生的,他有权决定讨论自由的限度。事实
上,政府此时代表的是大众。在这我们举了一个例子,是密
尔关于自由主义历史的。对自由惯有的理解现在已经脱离
了文本,在新的时代,旧的观念已经不再适用了。

　　早在 1859 年,密尔就提出民主应该再次成为审查公众 128
言论的标准。人们用旧的自由观念来反抗国王和贵族专制
统治。为什么一个大众选举的政府不能按照公众的要求限
制讨论自由呢? 为什么大臣依靠专用检查办法和安全性来
决定什么信息才能发布给公众呢? 例如,除非关系到切身
利益,公众真有兴趣知道关于石油短缺报告的细节吗? 这
一简单行为不会引起恐慌和危机吗? 公布北爱尔兰和平谈
判的信息真的是公众兴趣吗?

　　事实上,这些信息都有待讨论,在控制信息这一方面, 129
21 世纪的政府应该向先前的政府一样限制公众讨论,只是
应该少一点暴力措施。密尔并没有给任何问题做出明确的
答案。一份有关公众健康受到威胁的报告,当专家们还存
在分歧时,能不能公布呢? 这个问题从《论自由》中找不出
解决办法。但密尔鼓励人们对政府做出的审查结果进行质
疑,其中当然包括信息管理的审查。

　　密尔从 17 世纪到 19 世纪开始分析,对出版自由做出 130
了经典的论述。

# 五

# 聆听各家观点

131　　通过对书中的第二章的学习，我们详细地研究了密尔的"论思想自由和讨论自由"。通过分析我们知道密尔如何一个一个驳倒了"限制思想和讨论自由的原因"。整章都是在讨论这个问题。下面我们看一下密尔的自由原则、危害标准。

132　　这个方法引起了知识界不小的震动。在各种思想激烈冲突下，密尔对他的信条进行了推理。他的其他著作中，同样显示了他作为主要逻辑理论家的才能。《论自由》第二章中很好地证明了密尔非凡的思考艺术，有人称之为"观察全部思想的艺术"。

密尔思考的艺术

* 合理极端主义的方法。密尔要求我们从整体上理解这
  篇文章，而不是在我们自认为不错的地方就停下来。

* 辩证主义的方法。密尔要求我们从不同角度研究一个
  观点，也包括反对者的观点。思考就是考虑到每种反对
  观点的一门艺术。

如果我们不能始终遵循这种观点，或者我们不能考虑　133
到那些反对观点，我们就不能真正了解了这种观点。这是
理论推导的基本标准，密尔的实践就是最好的说明。

在整篇文章中，密尔要求我们聆听不同的观点，不管是　134
攻击性的、破坏性的观点，还是错误的疯狂的、怪异的、不相
关的观点。

## 纯化论者

纯化论者从不妥协。他们对生活有自己的观点，对每　135
个问题都有自己的答案。有些人认为"纯化论者"是一类与
他人毫无关联的人。我们要听他们的观点吗？我们可以以
一种非常礼貌的方式删除这种令人生气的观点吗？

## 极端主义者

极端主义者似乎对每个人都有攻击性。不管主流思想　136
是什么，极端主义者始终与之相反。他们使用的语言辛辣
讥讽，谩骂的词语比比皆是。极端主义者最鲜明的标志就

是大多数人认为是不好的、厌恶的观点,他们反而认为是好的。

## 偏执主义者

137　偏执主义者认为有阴谋在起作用。除了他们知道这个秘密外,其他人都被欺骗了。"偏执主义者"倾向于探讨一个问题,在主流人士看来,在所有的外行中,偏执主义者是唯一一种有理性的。

138　密尔的文章看起来更像是一段对话,尽管没有出现另外一个人的名字。我们就暂且称其为"普通人",它代表的是那些不认为听取他人观点重要的人的观点。"普通人"通常认为我们没必要去听取纯化论者、极端主义者或偏执主义者的意见,那样做只会使我们的讨论变复杂,也会曲解公众言论。他们使社会氛围变坏,他们转移大众注意力,使他们不能真正的关注一些重要的问题。我们决不应该和他们进行讨论。当然我们也不能把它们的思想封锁起来——尽管有时我们想这样做,因为我们还有许多其他方式能让他们缄默,至少不在公众讨论时提及。

139　在文章中,密尔想到了许多可以被普通人用于反对讨论自由的观点。

　　* 一致的观点:"每个人都同意!"

　　* 荒诞的观点:"我不想听这种废话!"

令人生气的观点:"那真是太可恶了!"

威胁性的观点:"那种观点动摇了文明社会的根基。"

自信的观点:"我们已经知道了事实"。

为了驳倒这些假设的观点,密尔不仅指出我们应该允 140
许异端人士及怪异思想的存在,而且我们绝对需要他们。

## 一致的观点:"每个人都同意!"

对普通人来说有一点是很明显的,当所有人都一致同 141
意一个观点时,就没有必要再听取反对意见了。自由讨论
也是有条件限制的,其中一条就是社会应该在哪些方面做
出决策。代表所有的极端主义者、纯化论者、偏执主义者以
及异端人士,密尔做出回应:

假定全体人类,除去一人之外,执有一种意
见,而仅仅一人执有相反的意见,这时,人类要
使那一人沉默并不比那一人(假如他有权力的话)要使人类沉
默较为正当。

摘录分析:

○ "除去一个人":密尔认为合理的极端主义者,异端
人士与法规同等重要。

○ "执有一种意见":人们所希望的一致性是公众意见

的一种理想形式。这是每位公众的共同目标。

142　　以"最后的马克思主义者"为例,他们是当代的纯理论者。没有人比他们更信奉马克思主义原则。我们都认为20年前冷战就已经结束了,我们真的有必要听他们无休止的谈论为什么阶级斗争仍然存在,为什么殖民主义是造成贫穷的原因? 社会能不能拒绝邀请"最后的马克思主义者"参与政党? 他可以中断所有的议程,回避质询时的提问,不再看出版物等等。用密尔的话说,这是绝对不正确的。我们既没有权力阻止"最后一个马克思主义者"讲话,也不能让其他人沉默。

143　　这里密尔同时引入了自由合理性试验和功利主义。如果这些"例外"没有危害,其他人没有权力阻止他发表自己的观点:这就是实行危害标准所产生的逻辑结果。引入功利主义为我们的研究提供了一个积极的视角:

　　　但是迫使一个意见不能发表的特殊罪恶乃在它是对整个人类的掠夺,对后代和对现存的一代都是一样,对不同意于那个意见的人比对抱持那个意见的人甚至更甚。

摘录分析:

○ "……对整个人类的掠夺":根据密尔为思想自由和讨论自由辩护来看,这是非常重要的一个阶段。如

果我们不让人们发表言论，我们就损害了人民的
利益。

○ "后代和现存的一代"：密尔把功利主义解释为作为
"进步个体"的人类追求的"永久利益"。这里他用
到了一条标准：思想永远存在，检举制度侵犯了人们
自己创造未来的权利。

举个例子，对我们大多数人来说，"极端主义者"最令人 144
讨厌的是他们认为自己是"唯一的人"，最后一个真正的人。
禁止说话真的侵犯人们权利吗？ 我们需要让他说一下自己
的发现吗？ 即人类已经没有了男性气质，或只有他有权做
自己想做的。密尔认为，人类需要倾听这种声音，不同的声
音："如果意见是正确的！"否则我们就会失去一个发现真理
的机会。但更为重要的是，如果意见是错误的：

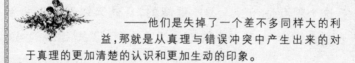

　　　　　　　——他们是失掉了一个差不多同样大的利
　　　益，那就是从真理与错误冲突中产生出来的对
于真理的更加清楚的认识和更加生动的印象。

摘录分析：

○ "冲突"：这是关于辩证法的一个陈述。观点只有不
断论证才能永恒。

○ "利益"："利益"和"成本"这两个词对分析和评价社
会保障有重要作用。

○ "印象"：这个词在英国哲学史和诗歌史上存在很久
了，包括密尔最喜欢的浪漫主义诗人华兹华斯的著
作中。印象就是短时间内留下的主观映象。

## 荒谬的观点："我不想听这种废话！"

145 普通人用许多观点来反驳自由讨论。为什么有些人必
须忍受一些看起来荒谬的观点的干扰呢？这就是除一致观
点之外的另一观点——荒谬观点。密尔运用了他的极端主
义思维来进行推理！

我们永远不能确信我们所力图窒闭的意见
是一个谬误的意见。

146 这个观点是一般人不能理解的，普通人以及他的哲学
代表们也许会问：我们真的不能确定这个观点是错误的吗？

147 偏执狂总是处于极端状态，当今社会中就有许多例子。
例如偏执狂认为联合国将取代美国，有人还是会卖被认为
不安全的食品。问题在于有时候偏执狂的确达到他们的目
标，进入了社会主流然后他们看起来会很高兴或失落。密
尔并没有说偏执主义者可能是对的，每个人都有自己思考
的空间。

148 就荒谬观点这一问题，密尔提出了经典的论述：

凡压默讨论,都是假定了绝对正确性。

摘录分析:

○ "绝对正确性":这个词最早产生于宗教和政治冲突,可以追溯到清教改革和天主教皇统治时期。关于宗教教条,教皇认为他的观点是绝对正确的。清教主义的产生也是出于对教皇专制统治的反抗。密尔认为,人们在无意识的情况下认为他们的观点是正确的,这是很正常的。"当你不允许别人讨论你的观点时,也许你认为自己的观点是完全正确的。"

○ "假定":现代逻辑学的一个重要作用就是揭示这种掩藏在普通观点下的假设,并对其提出质疑。逻辑学家总是对潜在的假设提出质疑。

实际上,密尔让检察官进行了自由合理性试验:如果一 149
个观点是荒谬的,它会产生什么危害呢? 他也求助于功利主义:

——所试图用权威而加以压制的那个意见可能是正确的。想要压制它的人们当然否认它的正确性,而那些人也不是绝对正确的。

150    这种观点比看上去更难理解。看到第一眼,他们会认为,这就是"自由相对论",即没有绝对真理,只有不同的观点。我们必须接受其他的观点,因为它们仅仅只是观点,都不是真理,因此人人都可以提出自己的观点。事实上,密尔并不是那种自由主义者。他是出于对真理的热爱才反对"绝对正确",并不仅仅只为接受不同观点。他对待真理非常认真,因为如果我们想看清一件事情的真相,就不能提前理解法院的观点。

151    真理是一个我们想要达到的限度,但我们永远达不到。虽然达不到,这个过程仍然非常重要。这是我们信任讨论的一个标志,也是我们承诺找出真理的标志。我们让所有的人都发表观点,即使那些人发表的观点看起来带有攻击性或破坏性。

152    这里,密尔不仅仅反对审查制度,他也准备了一些积极措施。可以说他为真正的讨论及真正的大众文化设定了标准。密尔允许其他人提出反对意见,如哪些观点听起来是"危险的"或是"可笑的"? 也许,从普通人的角度看,这两种观点能结合起来。他代表那些批评者提出质疑,是不是有些观点对人类利益有所伤害呢? 不管是对目前的生活还是其他? 在那个问题上,功利主义作为审查制度的基础,以另一种形式发挥作用。

**医学恐慌:虚构的事件**

153    现今,一些偏执极端主义者往往对一个事物极度的喜欢而对另一事物极度讨厌。他们四处宣传现代医药就是一个很大的阴谋。进行医学治疗是很不安全的,尤其不要让小孩子进行治疗。随着他们不断地宣传,父母变得越来越焦虑,他们尽量不带孩子去诊所,不接受医生的诊疗。有迹象表明这种行为引起了一种严重的流行病,婴儿的死亡率不断上升。为了我们的孩子,难道没有人反对这种观点吗?

专家们一致认为这场恐慌是由谎言、歪曲的事实和错 154
误的想法造成的。难道政府不能制止这种引起人们恐慌的行为吗? 应该有措施应对引起人们恐慌的这种错误的行为吧? 也许还应该有一些同样的不正当行为来反对这些人。也许媒体不应该给他们过多的报道。密尔认为我们应该直面这些问题,即使是与那些偏执极端主义者。当然,如果他们袭击诊所或给医生送恐吓信的话,那他就侵犯了人民自由,破坏了危害标准。但是如果他们真正谈到他们"疯狂的"行为时,我们又不得不同意他们的观点。原因就在于,在他们冗长的演说中,也许有些东西是真的,有些东西被我们忽视了。或者,我们可以找出我们为什么选择治疗而不是拒绝治疗的真正原因。

### BSE 丑闻：历史事件

你也许会说,那是空想出来的:它用理论解释了这种思 155
想,但在现实生活中我们却不能仅仅因为他们是危险的就检举这些愚蠢的争论。但是有许多方式可以让他们不发表言论。而且确实他们当中起着控制大众舆论的作用。

156　　　最近发生的 BSE 丑闻,是对密尔主要观点的一个经典的论述:首先,社会不允许公众发表令他们感到难堪的观点;其次,有许多方式可以禁止发表那些政府不想听到的观点;第三,即使在一些表面上比较科学的事件上,人们为什么也不能确定哪些是不重要的极端的观点呢? 在英国,当就人类传染病扩散发表第一个言论时,他们通常只是轻视对待。有一些观点专家们是不同意的,他们也面临着失去工作的危险或者他们已经失去了工作。媒体对这种先知者的报道也都是虚假的。这些都是现代审查制度最好的例证——我们回避厌恶观点的方法。这个事件也充分证明了密尔积极的观点,在这里他确实证明了有些东西,至少是那些难以理解的声明,我们应该认真对待。这些例子都证明了密尔的观点,自由主义和功利主义是分不开的。自由讨论是人们最关心的。

## 令人生气的观点:"那真是太可恶了!"

157　　　还有许多其他言论来审查言论是否自由。最著名的就是"可恶的观点"。有些代表主流文化的人声称个人或少数派让他们非常讨厌。

158　　　密尔不仅仅劝说人们忍受这种可恶的观点,他还在欢迎和鼓励人们发表观点。最后,这些争论把重点放在了侮辱神明的宗教和道德言辞上。为了阐释他的方法,他举了一个非常"棒"的例子:

即使牛顿的哲学体系,若未经允许加以质难,人类对它的正确性也不会像现在这样感到有完全的保证。

摘录分析：

○ "牛顿的哲学体系"：从 17 世纪起,牛顿的运动定律及万有引力定律被认为是科学界的权威。在本书中,牛顿学说代表了伟大真理,指明了社会发展的伟大前景。

○ "即使"：这并不是讨论万有引力的。"甚至"这个词把这个例子变成了"有限定的词"。密尔指的是社会认为"对不如牛顿的哲学思想以及那些完善的伟大真理提出质疑"是不受欢迎的。

一条伟大真理看起来越重要,就越有必要允许他人提 159 出质疑。原因在于如果没有人否认万有引力定律的话,它就不会有真正的含义。我们也不会真正地运用它。在这里,密尔举了一个例子,天主教堂允许恶魔对新提出的圣条质疑。伟大的真理都是这么产生的。

现在,密尔在讨论中引入了另一个词——"极端",在特 160 定的时间,自由主义应用到了极端主义观点中,并为之辩护。此时,他直接用"可恶的观点"来审查：

奇怪的是,人们既已承认自由讨论的论据的正确性,却又反对把这些论据"推至其极";他们没有看到,凡是理由,若不在极端的事情上有效,就不会在任何事情上有效。

摘录分析:

- ○ "承认…正确性":人们被迫接受没有被质难的观点。他们将可能否认《论自由》本章中得出的结论。

- ○ "极端":人们对自由讨论有一个理性的限度,但是他们却没有有效的论据去证明它。在这里,"极端"暗示了密尔考虑到了那些被认为是无理的、让人生气的、攻击主流思想的观点和思想。

161　　因此,密尔认为如果一个社会能够认真对待自由讨论这件事,它会积极鼓励人们发表一些不太受欢迎的思想。他与"普通人"相对立。在"普通人"看来,有些观点是不允许人们质疑的。如果怀疑就是犯罪:只有坏人才要削弱那些有益的信条。

162　　在当今社会,"家庭价值"和"工作是对人们有益的"等都是伟大的真理。那些质疑家庭价值的辱骂性的描述,都是一种滥用,密尔称之为审查制度的一种形式。在本文中,密尔认为亵渎神明的言词和异教言论都是有益的:它们对已经证实的假设提出质疑,如果不那样的话,就没有改变的余地了。他就可恶的观点举了一个宗教方面的例子：

把所要论驳的意见定为对上帝或彼界的信仰，或者任何一个一般公认的道德方面的教义。

上帝和道德融为一体。对这些神圣的教条提出质疑仅 163
仅在道德上不能接受吗？神圣的教条为极端主义者提供了
大量的材料，没有一条信条不受到激烈的批评。当然，这很
容易引起信仰者的反感，不管他们信仰的是上帝、家庭还是
异性交往。毕竟，那些被认为是极端主义者的人可以根据
别人的看法做出改变。第一位伟大的哲学家苏格拉底就是
因为颠覆了已经确立的道德教条而被判处死刑。"向人类
提醒从前有过一个名叫苏格拉底的人这件事总难嫌其太频
吧"。

让人高兴的是，耶稣本身也是一个很好的例子： 164

这个人，凡曾看到他的生活和听到他谈话
的人都在记忆上对于他的道德之崇高伟大留有
这等印象，以致此后十八个世纪以来人们都敬奉为万能上帝的
化身。他竟被卑劣地处死了。当作什么人呢？当作一个亵渎
神明的人。

在此，密尔更加认为这种亵渎神明的行为是处理功利 165
主义积极观点的。如果我们把目光放长远，回顾一下历史，

我们就会意识到我们不能确定一个人或他的观点是怎样产生的。历史上有创造力的大人物往往被他所处的时代认为是亵渎神明者,这也是合乎情理的。简单地说,那些观点引起了社会的变革和进步,但对当时的社会来说是令人生气的。不过又能怎样呢?

166     这里再一次证明了为自由辩护的基础是辩证历史主义。我们需要不同的观点来反对现存的正教,否则,人们将会变得麻木。我们自己不能决定当今社会中哪种极端主义者会推动人类进步,而哪些又是让人讨厌的。事实上,大多数情况下极端主义者只是让人痛苦的。问题在于有时只有他们才呼唤新时代的到来。

167     用令人生气的观点来进行裁判这也是十分危险的。首先,密尔认为应该排除极端主义者危害自由合理性试验这种观点。他们除了冲击了主流思想以外,并没有"伤害其他人"。第二,同样也是很重要的一点,密尔运用了功利主义原则。最终看来,极端主义长期致力于人类的发展。没有人想到这种无理的观点竟然会发展为历史上的功利主义。

**威胁性的观点:"那种观点动摇了文明社会的根基。"**

168     那些价值观念对社会存亡来说是必不可少的吗?维多利亚时期的批评家詹姆斯·史蒂芬非常生气:他说,很明显,社会必须保护其基本价值观不受危害。密尔认为,这些问题来源于先前讨论的异教观点。例如罗马帝国的皇帝马库斯·奥里利乌斯认为基督教会颠覆文明的罗马社会,于是他对其进行了残酷的镇压。

 ——可是他看到,或者他想他看到,这世界是借着信奉已经公认的神道而得维持在一起并免于变得更糟的。

摘录分析:

○ "借着信奉……维持在一起":这是一个常见的假设:某些信条把社会维持在一起。哪里用到这些信条,哪里的社会整体就凌驾于自由。

○ "已经公认的神道":在罗马时期异教的神控制着社会主要的机关。在这之后,就出现了许多不同的教条:国家、君主专制。

马库斯·奥里利乌斯大帝是一个高尚的人,一个真正 169
的哲学家。但是他反对自由,因为他认为自由是"公开的破坏这种联系"。这就是威胁性的观点。有些观点是很不好的,因此社会不允许完全的讨论自由。

为异教徒辩护后,密尔又抨击了这种威胁性的观点,但 170
总的来说,这些持有破坏性的观点的人本身也有自己的信仰。为了使主流思想引导他们的思想,这些被认为是异教徒的人必须设立一条更高的文明标准。

——每个时代中，大部分持异端思想的人都非常正直和光荣。

171 威胁性的观点主要是让人害怕，不管是多数派还是异教徒。我们站在社会边缘。我们是一个整体，坚信保证那些能使我们安全的信条。在这种压抑的环境下，少数派一般保持沉默，不再发表他们的观点：

凡认为异端者的这种缄默不算一种灾害的人，首先应当思量一下——这样缄默的结果是使异端意见永远得不到公平透彻的讨论。

摘录分析：

○ "缄默"：仅仅使人们在讲话时迟疑就足以压制自由讨论。审查制度毕竟是审查制度。

○ "公平透彻"：只有公平透彻讨论才可以避免异端意见。如果外行人遭到拒绝，他们不会从中学到什么。如果我们不试着接纳他们，那我们永远不知道主流思想的限度是什么。

172 密尔就社会凝聚力和自由讨论提出了重要的两点：

1. 没有部分自由的讨论。

　　2．功利主义从来没有镇压过任何一个观点。威胁性的观点建议如果某些观点不发表，社会作为一个整体应该会更好。但密尔反驳说产生的作用对双方——审查人员和被审查人员——都不会很好。

## 自信的观点：“我们已经知道了事实”。

　　当然，如果我们所说的都是真的，就没必要去听其他人　173的意见了吗？密尔进行了一系列的讨论企图推翻这些表面上似乎合理的、具有常识的观点。他提出了许多生动的公式让我们重新认识“真实的”和“真理”：

　　　　　　　　普遍意见……经常是对的，但很少或者从
　　　　　来不是全部的真理……所以只有借敌对意见的
冲突才能使所遗真理有机会得到补足。

　　密尔的讨论主要是关于真理和历史。　　　　　　　　　174

* 敌对意见有时能反映真理的另一面，而这一面在一
　段时间内被人们忽视了。

* 真理是辩证的：它包括与敌对势力不停的争斗。斗
　争就是不断地阻挠了解实情的真相。

　　密尔认为在特定的时间内，敌对意见对了解真理十分　175重要。我们所了解的真理往往不如我们不了解的那一面更

有用。"真理的另一面往往更吸引人,更能满足时代需求。"

176　　密尔试图让我们更全面地了解真理,它比我们传统上想象的要更广泛。他的论述被喻为 19 世纪对时间的伟大发现。之前,时间被局限于人类活动的时期:地球和宇宙都是人类可以理解的内容。但是,维多利亚时期地理学和生物学不再是狭隘的把时间认为是达尔文《物种起源》中所说的深度时间。密尔要求人们修正对真理的理解,认识到真理是非常有深度和广泛的,它涉及许多反方面,这是远远超出想象的。

177　　密尔对基督教的道德规范也做了详细的研究。他们是确有根据的,但是不完整的。最初,基督教表达了那种异端思想——被古典的道德规范掩藏的真理。古典道德规范认为必须为社会服务,他们忽视了个人的救赎:"基督教道德规范包括或仅仅包括真理的一部分。"

178　　我们一般把道德规范认为是一种主张,但密尔把不同的道德体系看作是对辩证的研究真理的贡献。关于这一点,他的思想与维多利亚时期另一自由主义思想家马修·阿诺德非常相似,阿诺德对希伯来语和希腊语进行了区分。

179　　密尔认为他讨论的目标就是"让人们得到精神幸福。"幸福是下一章讲的主要内容。

# 六

# 做自由的人:

# 密尔关于幸福的名言

　　《论自由》第三章是"论个性"。在导读的这一部分,我　180
们将会了解到为什么密尔把个性称为人类幸福的因素之
一。正如当时的哲学家希拉里·普特南所说,每篇论文都
适可而止。即便是复杂的逻辑思维也有完结的时候,也有
理性思维解释不了的一个点。在密尔看来,这个点就是"个
性"。也许你会问,自由的那个点是什么呢?运用理性思维
给出的答案就是:自由使我们成为个体,成为我们自己。

　　密尔的讨论已经进入到了另一个阶段,他采取了一种　181
新的方式。前一章,他用理性的语气写道:

    \* 使各种思想相互交融；

    \* 对各种思想提出反驳的观点。

182    而在这一章中，他用了另一种语气，使文章更容易被读者接受。这就是如同格言的话语。第三章满是谚语、格言或类似的东西。有时，这一章更像是奥斯卡·王尔德在说教，而不像出自一个哲学家之口。为什么密尔用这种方式来写作呢？他的理性推导已经到了末端。这一章并不是一个随意的声明，它也与理性思维有关，但其中不乏感性的说教。这些格言都朴实无华。因此，密尔自然而然地以"最后的呼声"的方式表达了他的思想。同时，尽管这些格言都是含蓄陈述，它们也极易引起人们的共鸣。但持有传统观念的人仍然认为它们就像王尔德或尼采书中所写的那样，是充满暴虐的。

## 个性和幸福

183    看一看这一章的题目"论个性为人类幸福的因素之一"。在文章结尾，密尔没有通过道德和政治为个性辩护。整篇文章升华到人类幸福这个理论高度。

> **自由的基础**
> 个性的自由发展乃是康乐的首要要素之一。

184    这里体现了一条清晰的思路。没有自由，我们就不是我们自己，甚至不能找到什么是真正的自我。而幸福即尽可能地做你自己。什么会反对人类幸福呢？密尔认为传统的价值观念危害了人类幸福，因为他们抑制个性的表达。许多人从道德角度来看待人类的生活状况，即人们采用一些外在的固定的标准来评判什么才是幸福的生活，什么才是最好的生活方式。《论自由》发动了一场反对道德教条的文化战争。

　　密尔对自由的看法仍然是激进的，因为它是人类幸福　185
的因素之一，扫清了道德观念的影响。没有人能告诉你，什么让你获得幸福。密尔指出"个性"这个词与一致性是相对的。在上一章中我们讲到，他认为讨论自由辩护是基于讨论多样性的基础上。为了社会健康发展，我们需要听取不同的意见和观点，只有在矛盾和不断比较中文化才能不断进步。真理允许不同的思想相互碰撞。现在，他又把这种辩证看问题的方法运用到了研究个人生活中。

> **自由的逻辑**
> 　　如果只有培养个性才产生出发展得很好的人类，那么一致性将阻碍人类发展。

　　纵观全文，我们就密尔的功利主义理论及如何把它与　186
自由联系在一起等提出了许多问题。在论个性发展问题上，密尔既拥护自由主义，也支持功利主义。从功利主义对幸福的解释中我们可以看出，人类幸福是一个更微妙更人性化的词。自由是好的,因为它有利于人类幸福,在宣传真正幸福与痛苦环节它是很有用的。

187　　接下来,在这本"关于人类幸福的字典"中,我们选取了其中几条非常著名的格言。

## 密尔关于幸福的名言

关于幸福的第一条格言

人们应当有自由去依照他们的意见而行动。

密尔关于幸福的字典

- "有自由":指的是人们可以依照其意见而行动。仅仅持有或表达其意见是远远不够的。因此,意见自由还应包括自由地依照意见行动。

- "可以自由的……"与"不受……"同等重要。实际上,我们可以说"对…的自由"是"不受…"的结果。行为不受干扰指的就是可以自由地行动。有关人类幸福的格言都是"可以自由地……"——而先前则是"不受……"。

- "他们的意见":如果一个人不能把他的意见付诸于行动,我们就不能说他拥有这种意见。

## 含　意

### 真实性

如果意见的持有人不能付诸其行动的话，那么这条意 188
见就是不真实的。密尔是一个充满理性的思想家，他倾向
于把尼采及 D.H. 劳伦斯等人的浪漫主义思想与真实性连
接在一起。正如我们看到的，他要求真实，这正是维多利亚
时期文人们所反对的，这看起来有点虚伪。如果禁止人们
行动我们就会变得虚伪。再过一段时间，社会中的人们就
不清楚他们之间是否真诚，是否完全相信他们的建议或只
是在装腔作势。

### 意见的科学性

这则格言也有其科学性的一面。如果你不能依照意见 189
行动，这就像把科学简单地认为是一种假设——你不想去
证明他们。但事实上，意见也是一种假设，道德上的、心理
上的又或是政治上的假设等。行动是检验假设的最好工
具。如果我不能依照意见行动，那我就被剥夺了拒绝它的
权力。

## 条　件

密尔认为一条格言必须具备两方面的条件： 190

1. 积极的正面的。阻碍行动自由主要有两方面的因
　　素：身体上的和道德上的。如果我们为自己的生活

做好了准备,我们就不应受到这些东西的阻碍。道德限制与身体上的限制没有什么不同,这种消极的道德观念是限制他人生活的一种方式。道德束缚也变成了一种监狱。

2. 消极的反面的。密尔强调,人们自由地依照其意见行动并对其负责。这已成为那时社会和道德思想中的一种强烈趋势。在密尔看来,风险和自由是一体的,每个自由的个体都有自己的生活,如果你不能承担风险,你就不是一个自主的个体:这也正是孩子与大人之间的差别。

191　　　一个自由的社会不能排除人们生活中的风险,没有风险,也就没有个性。社会不会让人们过完全无风险的生活。

关于幸福的第二条格言

当人类尚未完善时…人生应当有多种不同的试验。

密尔关于幸福的字典

○ "尚未完善":这里有一种讽刺的意味:人类还能变成什么样?最重要也是最关键的一点就是:人类是不断进化的,他们只会比现在更趋于完善。不管怎样,人类需要多样性:这也是不断产生变化的原因。

○ "试验"：这里把我们的生活比作了科学研究。每个
自由的个体都对美好的生活有自己的设想。而那种
生活就像科学实验，他们在试验中检验理论。正如
通过实验科学可以消除错误，有新的发现。"实验
性"也充分体现了一些新的原创的东西：与先前的
"风险"也有一定关联。

## 含 意

在一个自由社会，选择哪种生活也是一个辩证的过程，192
是不同生活观念之间的竞争。每个人对自己的生活方式做
出选择，不同的生活方式间就产生竞争。这种竞争促进了
人类历史的发展。不久，人们会发现，这种选择是好的，而
另一种则是不好的。密尔认为这些"试验"是非常有用的：
他把功利主义运用到了个人选择当中。如果个体可以尝试
不同的生活方式，那么对整个人类都是有益的。尽管有些
人会有所收获，有些人会失去一些东西，但整个人类会越来
越好。如果人们都可以尝试不同的生活方式，这样不断地
累计，人类幸福也会越来越多。

历史是唯一可以对人们选择做出合理判断的事物。哪 193
种生活方式被证明对人类有益？

关于幸福的第三条格言

要按照他自己的方法去运用和解释经验，这是人的特权，也是人的正当的条件。

## 密尔关于幸福的字典

○ "这是人的特权，也是人的正当的条件"：密尔在对自由的论述中并没有用到"权利"这个概念。他并没有认为获得自由是人类的一种权利，但他认为人们应该有一个"恰当地适用于他自己的情况"，即自由。"情况"这个词最早用于医学：处于良好的状况即身体健康。这种良好的状况也是人类幸福的一部分。密尔认为，即便我们没有权利，我们也可以在一定环境下表达我们的想法。在本文的语境下，"特权"这个词有讽刺意味。没有人给予我们人类特权：这是出于我们人类自身。

○ "解释"：解释已成为现代思想中的一个基本主题。例如他是弗洛伊德理论的主题，开始于《梦的解析》。我们自己来解释我们的生活。解释可以把发生在我们身上的事转化成我们的经验。通过解释，我们可以更好地了解生活。我们用"自己"的思想来解释生活。密尔把"运用"和"解释"联系起来：解释并不奇怪也不抽象。如果我们不能解释我们的生活,我们就不会运用它。

## 含 意

如果人类自己解释他们的生活,那他们都是"自反"地  194
看问题。密尔认为,我们所说的自由包括有足够的空间让
我们自我反省。这与其后的许多思想家观点一致。其中也
包括当今社会很有影响力的一些,如著名的社会学家安东
尼·吉登斯和提出"风险社会"的理论家乌尔里希·贝
克等。

现在,密尔的声望正在不断上升。这些都是后现代主  195
义中自由的标准。就人类幸福这一理论,密尔成为后现代
自由主义教条的先驱。因此,在当代社会,他关于言论自由
的理论成为《论自由》中最具影响力和争议性的一部分,他
的个性理论也成为后现代主义时期最有影响力的思想。密
尔的《论自由》把自反性看作是人类幸福的一部分。根据自
由合理性试验,它没有伤害任何人,根据功利主义来看,它
为人们经验提供了更多的可能性,因此,它是合理的。

> **密尔和后现代的自由主义**
> 我们必须自由地解释我们的生活。自由具有自反性。

关于幸福的第四条格言

他人的传统和习俗,在某种程度上,乃是表明他们的经验教过他们什么东西的验证。

密尔关于幸福的字典

○ "传统和习俗":密尔把传统和习俗解释为对经验的二次翻译。在某种程度上,我们遵循传统和习俗,我们过着模仿他人的生活。传统和习俗可以帮助我们解释经验。更好一点,如果从外界看来,别人的传统和习俗在我们解释自己的生活时是很有帮助的。因此,他们帮助我们构筑经验:他是如何帮助我们理解自己的生活的呢?

**条 件**

196 密尔认为这种传统和习俗体现了一个人正确理解别人的经验。换句话说,他不是那种把所有传统和习俗都看成是错误的思想家。密尔并不是一个未开化的现代人。他并不因为传统和习俗很古老就认为他们是不好的,也不认为新产生的那些就很好。他的结论就是某些人从自身的经验和角度出发,认为传统和习俗是好的。但这些在我们的新生活中仍然需要检验。对传统和习俗原来的理解是正确的,但不一定适合每个人。

## 含　意

密尔并不反对风俗和习惯。他反对的是那些被强制执 197
行的习俗或那些即将突破道德界限的传统。如果社会强制
实行某些习俗,那么这些习俗要求人们按照某种特定的方
式去理解。为什么每一代人都要按照自己对他们祖先的理
解生活呢？换句话说,密尔认为如果人们只考虑自己,这些
严格的习俗就会剥夺人们可能产生某些新的想法。

例如,过去一些人通过引诱经历了性生活,而另一些人 198
通过自我表现来获得性生活。社会是团结合作的,而我们
是单独生活的。你的离开给我创造了机会。你的离题给我
创造了新的世界。按照密尔的话说,两方不可能相互转换,
只有一种正确的解释。并没有正确的答案,在不伤害他人
的前提下,问题在于哪种解释"适合"我。

关于幸福的第五条格言
因为习惯而照着办事的人不会作任何
选择。

密尔关于幸福的字典

○ "选择"：在当代政治和道德争论中,"选择"已经成
为一个主要的概念。下面的例子是关于密尔对现在
与未来的联系的讨论。他解释了这个我们十分关注

的词语。密尔认为,选择是个性的一个功能。一个真正的选择表达了我们的本性,但不表达我们属于的那种方式。

○ "不作任何选择":密尔提出了关于错误的和非真实选择的理论。一个基于习俗基础上的社会会减弱或消除真正的选择。如果人们在传统的基础上做出选择,那他们就不能成为真正的个体。

**含　意**

\* 所有的选择都是个人的。

\* 一个人有越多的选择意味着个性越能充分发挥。

199　　按照普通标准来看,这些观点都很极端。人们忽视这些平常的判断标准和要求的频率是多少呢?我们没有考虑任何标准就做出选择的机会有多少呢?密尔认为,做出真正的选择是很困难的。

200　　现代政治家和经济学家经常谈论扩大选择以及给予人们更多的选择。密尔认为大多数选择都有欺骗性的。让他接受"顾客选择"这种传统观念他是不会高兴的,例如大多数情况下顾客在设定的限度下进行选择——如广告所说的时尚、社会地位或价值观念等。依照密尔的标准,目前的生活方式不比传统的生活方式更好。事实上,生活方式只是一种简单的短暂的习俗。

201　　密尔认为人们如果只是根据惯例做出选择,我们就不能把他们生活的社会称为自由的社会。同样,如果人们只是根据广告宣传买一些东西,那么这种社会也不是自由的社会。下面是一个关于生小孩的例子。密尔认为,如果人们生小孩只是因为他们应该这么做,那么他们真的就是无法选择。

关于幸福的第六条格言

欲望和冲动确是一个完善人类的构成部分,与信赖和约束居于同等地位。

密尔关于幸福的字典

○ "欲望和冲动":密尔又一次预见了弗洛伊德和现代的心理学发展。抑制欲望只会使我们更不像人,更没有教养。缺乏冲动则会使我们麻木,遇事也不会沉着冷静。

○ "一个完善的人类":这是一个理想,不是一个解决方案。密尔支持和维护人类生活的某些方式,而反对另一些,他不认为我们最终会达到完善,但他有自己的一套判断标准。密尔认为,所谓的完善应该是尽可能全面地表达人们的本性——在不伤害他人的前提下,表达得越多越好。

**含 意**

密尔也是从辩证的角度来看待幸福的。他不认为人类 202 所有的欲望都是好的,我们也不应该冲动行事。相反的,他认为一个人必须拥有欲望和信仰、冲动和抑制冲动。在讨论这个问题时,信仰指的是组成论述的相关观点和判定标准以及其他方面的内容。欲望是个人一致的瞬间表达,本能的动力。只有把欲望和信仰、冲动和抑制冲动联系在一起,才能实现真正的自我节制。一个没有欲望的人根本没有自我节制能力:首先,他们要节制什么呢?

203　　密尔并不认为强烈的冲动具有危险性,只在它没有恰当地得到平衡的时候,才会产生问题。没有强烈欲望的人不可能形成真正的自我节制。为什么他们必须这样呢? 因为自控能力和欲望共同组成了人的经验。

204　　从这里我们看出,密尔有时是一个相对论者,有时又不是。他不想把一个好人的模型强加于他人,这一点上他是一个相对论者。但当他为某种可以让人们生活得更好的生活方式辩护时,而这种方式是建立在"一个完善的人类"——在不伤害他人的前提下,尽可能全面的表达人性的每一面——这种思想上时,他又不是一个相对论者。人类越是接近完善,人类历史上我们生活的效用值就会越大。

关于幸福的第七条格言
强欲望与弱良心这二者之间没有任何自然的联系。

密尔关于幸福的字典

○ "良心":通读《论自由》全书,我们可以发现密尔反
对对人们实施训诫。大多数人的道德观不仅可以判
断他人行为的是否标准,也合理地说明了他们为什
么不喜欢那些与众不同的大胆的让人尴尬的东西。
密尔对什么是真正的有道德的良心有自己的一套理
论,即一种可以和冲动平衡的力量。真正的良心是
一个很私人的东西。欲望也一样。欲望和抑制欲望
二者用后现代主义的语言表达了我们对生活的幻想
和自己的计划。

○ "强"和"弱":力量就是一个人的一种能力和存在方
式。密尔认为所有的存在因素都有可能聚集起来变
大或缩小。因此,抑制并不是促进增长的好方法。
如果你反对某人的某方面,你就缩小了他存在的全
部空间。因此,弱也是人类的一种能力。

密尔用到了性格强和弱,而不是特性强和弱。在这一 205
方面,他的方法与 19 世纪德国哲学家尼采的非常相似。

**含 意**

密尔提出了关于幸福的另一条理论,即冲突。如果社 206
会企图从外部控制我们的欲望,我们就不会体会到这种欲
望和良心之间的冲突。一个抑制欲望的社会同样会摧毁良
心存在的可能性。生活在一个不允许人们有冲动和欲望的

社会,人们也不会有良心,更不会有合乎伦理的生活。新的道德观与新的欲望一起产生。那些发现道德的人们内心生活也是很丰富的,充满着强烈的冲动。他们努力寻找新的平衡。

207　　情感丰富的人并不意味着理性思维差。最富于自然情感的人往往也会有丰富的理性。密尔的个性理论主要强调完整性。

> **密尔与现代心理学**
> 　　幸福意味着完整性。越是完整,人们越是幸福。我们人类是在冲突中不断成长的。

208　　有人批评密尔只用反面的方法研究自由,但当放在幸福理论下时,这种谴责看起来很不公平。自由是一种状态,有可能成为人类最大幸福。密尔对人类幸福也有一个全面的理解。他想要创造一种新的语言来解读道德审查和传统权威的主张。密尔不仅仅是反权威,而且他坚信人的独立性。

209　　有人批评密尔没有把他的自由主义理论与功利主义哲学联系在一起。这句话放在就个性的论述的语境下时,也是不公平的。他的功利主义使他同时是一个自由主义者——他把自由看作是最大限度提高人们兴趣的最佳状态。

# 七

# 实用自由主义

本章中,我们将研究密尔是如何把各部分联合起来讨 210
论的。在《论自由》后半部分,主要讨论了当时社会中的一
些问题以及一些具体的建议和驳论。从第三章(论个性)结
尾到第四章(论社会驾于个人的权威的限度)以及第五章
(本文教义的应用),作者进行了较为实用的论述。尽管每
一章节都叙述得生动且富有激情,但却丝毫没有改变观点,
也没有向我们介绍新的内容。

现在,密尔开始讲到了实际应用。也许把这部分的理 211
论应用到我们现在社会中研究更合适。这些观点现在仍然
应用于许多方面。有些一般概念仍然起作用,但《论自由》
中最实用的观点都已经过时了。

## "倡导自由"运动

212    2001 年 1 月 10 日星期三,英国 BBC 新闻报道:

> 陪审团一致宣判一名老练的裸体主义运动者有碍公益。

213    这个人就是文森特·贝塞尔,"倡导自由"运动的组织者和主要领导人。为了反对政府对公众任意强加的要求,他裸体上台以示抗议,当时,地方法官判定这一行为有罪。这是他的第一次审判,十名男性和两名女性陪审员宣判他有罪。在法庭上,贝塞尔声称:"回归人性并没有犯罪。"法官警告他不要太主观了:"关于那个问题,我不想考虑的太多,虽然在当今社会环境下,那并没有妨碍社会公益。"

214    事情报道后的第二天,英国的全国性综合日报《卫报》这样写道:"第一个裸体站在英国法庭上接受审判的人。"

215    《论自由》中也有对这一事件进行的分析。难道这个古怪的人不能选择他的身份? 或者,他伤害到其他人? 法庭上,原告声称他的这一行为"伤害了公众的道德观念并让他们感到不舒服,或阻挠某公众行使他们的权利"。参与"争取自由运动"(《卫报》,1999 年 7 月 28 日)的人认为在"不论性别裸体示威"中,并没有伤害任何人。其中有一段小插曲,一次贝塞尔赤身站在一根灯柱上,一位过路人看到后作出评论:"旁观者看到有人抗议并不震惊,因为抗议者并没有伤害任何人。"这句话后来成为一句格言。

　　从这个故事中我们除了看到了好的一面,也看得出其　216
中不好的一面。在审判之前贝塞尔曾被关在伦敦南部的布
瑞克斯顿监狱两个月,因为身为一个在押犯,他拒绝穿
囚衣。

　　　他打电话告诉我们他赤裸着身体,日日夜夜地被

　　关在这个 11 英尺乘 7 英尺的小房间里……没有人来

　　探视。他说,之所以不让别人来探视是为了不吓到他

　　们,而没有户外活动是避免弄伤他的脚。

　　　　　　　　　　　　　　　　《卫报》2000 年 9 月 9 日

　　密尔是怎样把自由讨论和这件事联系起来的?　在"本　217
文教义的应用"一章中,密尔勉强地加了一些对举止言行方
面的评论,他指出《论自由》没有讨论有伤体统的言行,而是
涉及另一个更广的问题——自我表达。他说有"许多行为"
适合私下做,而不适合公众场合。他的语气严谨,称这些有
伤体统的言行会"破坏良好的风气"。他认为那种行为应当
叫停。由于厌恶和尴尬,密尔认为"这些行为有失体统,因
此没有必要仔细讨论。"

　　密尔并没有参与"倡导自由"运动。事实上,他认为这　218
项运动是对自由主义思想的滑稽模仿,是很危险的。同时,
如果他的确反对贝塞尔的行为,他也许会认为他"破坏良
好的风气",而不是"违反了社会道德"。很明显,他们的时
代有良好的生活方式;他们可以改变,但相应的行为限度也

会改变。看起来不可能因为一个人的行为不当就把他关起来。到目前为止,密尔的语言始终比现在的道德辩论更精炼文雅。

219　　其他的文章至少会使我们给予这些运动法律许可时犹豫不决。密尔惋惜地说"个性已经在尘嚣中消失。"他积极地评价说:

　　　　因为意见的暴虐已达到把反叛当成一个谴责对象的地步,所以为了突破这种暴虐,人们的反叛才更为可取。

220　　不穿衣服就被认为是不可取的怪癖? 有人曾认为论公共得体行为的文章太过严谨,但密尔并不这么认为。他提出了另一问题。不是简单地对这些行为有没有造成伤害好奇,我们也想知道是否有可能真有可取的怪癖。在这个强调同一性的社会,这个人是否被误导了,把"自立"和"无礼的行为"混淆了?《论自由》并不打算回答这些问题。写这本书的目的是让我们提出更多的疑问,使用更精练的词语,这些也都贯彻执行在社会后来的发展过程中。

221　　裸体示威运动很好地说明了这样一个事实:密尔在第四章"论社会驾于个人的权威的限度"中提出的问题也是我们的问题。

这样讲来,个人统治自己的主权又以什么
为正当的限制呢?

　　密尔的论述始终激发我们不断地提出这个问题,文章　222
不是让我们不经思考地接受一些观点,而是不断地提出问
题。也许"倡导自由"运动的参加者违反了社会道德,我们
应该禁止这种行为。但是我们不能通过"强加管制"这种行
为来表达我们的厌恶,因为这种方式太严厉。

　　密尔并不希望有这样的一个"坚定沉着"的世界,生活　223
在里面的人们都无视他人的存在,都日复一日地过着枯燥
乏味的生活。我们也许应该寻找一种更人道的方式来表达
我们的不满,虽然我们认为这个人的行为并没有造成任何
伤害,但他却始终不符合相应的标准:

　　　　我在这里所争论的一点是,一个人若只在
　　　　涉及自己的好处而不影响到与他发生关系的他
人的利益的这部分行为和性格上招致他人观感不佳的判定,他
因此而应承受的唯一后果只是与那种判定密切相连的一些不
便。至于对他人有损害的行动,那就需要有完全不同的对
待了。

　　我们很可能控制他们,不让他们再做出类似的行为。　224
但是我们有时也应该忍受他们的行为,把它当作是必要的

"观感不佳"：

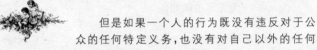

> 但是如果一个人的行为既没有违反对于公
> 众的任何特定义务，也没有对自己以外的任何
> 个人发生什么觉察得到的伤害，而由这种行为产生出来对社会
> 的损害也只是非必然或者可以说是推定的性质，那么，这一点
> 点的不便利，社会为着人类自由的更大利益之故是能够承受
> 的。假如说成年的人因不能正当地照管自己而应受惩罚，我宁
> 愿说这是为他自己之故。

225    你也许认为不穿衣服是"没有照顾好某人的"表现。但
事实上监狱方面把这个当作反对贝塞尔户外锻炼的借口：
他在院子里可能伤到脚。我们也许好奇，为什么院子不为
他建得安全一点呢？这使我们不再相信他们所给出的那些
理由。

226    密尔使我们认清了限制"个人统治的主权"是多么严重
的一件事。每当我们想要阻止他人时，例如"倡导自由"活
动的参与者，我们都侵害了他们的自由权。如果我们真的
觉得他的行为破坏了社会得体的生活环境，我们那一行为
还说得过去，但我们必须尽量避免干预他们，我们必须诚实
地履行我们的动机。他们的无礼言行真的难以忍受吗？还
是我们因为他们与我们不一样而生气：

有很多人把他们所厌恶的任何行为看作对
自己的一种伤害,愤恨它好像它对于他们的情
感是一种暴行。

　　我们也许需要很讨厌这些,但它的确没有对我们造成　227
伤害——或许是我们由于自己的过激行为或缺乏控制自己
感情的能力而伤害了自己?《论自由》丰富和美化了我们在
表达对他人不得体行为不满时所说的话语。

## 必须保持缄默? 密尔和揭发者

　　1999 年 3 月 16 日,星期二,整个欧洲因为这条宣言而　228
震惊:

　　昨晚,欧洲解体了,因为整个欧盟委员会签署了独
立委员会提出的一份绝佳的报告。

　　　　　　　　　　　　　　　　　　　　《卫报》

　　欧盟委员会主席雅克·桑特昨夜刚刚参加了一个
激动人心的会议。

　　　　　　　　　　　　　　　　　　　BBC 新闻

　　这则消息令人非常震撼,它影响到整个世界,标志着欧　229
盟集权制统治的解体。英国广播公司这样评价道:

随着20个成员国的退出,欧盟陷入了一场危机,其前景目前还不明确。

230 　　所有的这些都是由欧盟的一个名叫保罗·万·布侬特南的荷兰会计师引起的。早在1998年,这名官员写了一份国内报道,详细地说明了欧盟的骗局和管理不当。以防被禁止发表,他向欧洲议会绿党提交了一份副本。然而,他被停职并且薪水减半。报告中指出当政府官员因受贿被起诉时,应予以停职但工资照旧。

231 　　绿党发表了这篇文章,1998年2月17日欧盟议会不再相信欧盟委员会。起初委员会故意推迟和否认这件事,但最后,欧盟委员会主席雅克·桑特承认确实有许多违法乱纪的行为发生。

232 　　政府开始调查此事。同时,保罗·万·布侬特南因"将消息告知未经认可和不适宜的人"而被起诉。英国广播公司1999年1月6日报道:

　　　委员会宣布,他因未经批准将调查详情公布于众这一行为违反合约,于是停职。

233 　　一名欧盟发言人解释说:"事情正在调查过程中时,这份报告应该保密。"同时,"揭发者"也因此出名,面临来自各方的压力。1999年1月11日《卫报》对此事的报道:公开地宣称他是个疯子。说他是一个狂热的宗教徒一个政治极端分子:

我承认我的部分动机是出于我是一个基督教徒…
我没意识到我的这种行为是违法的。他们说我是右翼
分子…而我是绿党的一员。

《卫报》,1999 年 10 月 13 日

当公布调查报告时,由于特殊原因,万·布依特南的索 234
赔已经得到了批准。

事实上,密尔认为是人们自己限制了自己行为自由和 235
表达自由的权利。揭发者是否应该遵守这些合约条款,在
官方调查完之前严守秘密呢? 密尔认为,他签署原来的工
作约定,是经过双方同意的,并且:

> ……而当他们这样做了之后,照一般规律
> 来说,就宜遵守那个约定。可是,或许在每个国
> 度的法律中,这个一般规律也有某些例外……不仅不责成人们
> 遵守那种违犯第三方面的权利的定约,就是某种定约有害于双
> 方自己时,这有时也足可成为叫他们解除那个定约的充分
> 理由。

换句话说,我们必须遵守契约,当然也有某些例外。人 236
们不应该被这些约定束缚而拒绝行使他们最基本的自由
权,反对他人的真正利益或伤害自己。欧盟认为意见不同
者应该停职,因为他们违反了约定,但密尔特别指出,不可
能永远"履行契约"。

拥有表达自由权和个性时会不利于人们"履行"和约条 237

款。例如,我们认为如果没有发表这条消息,就损害了欧洲公民的利益。我们也可以说万·布依特南为了个人的利益也必须揭发消息:它可以经得住反对者的压力吗?

238    密尔的很多论述似乎都围绕着这一著名的事件。消息的揭发是表达自由的一个表现,它可以在更大范围上为人们的"永久利益"服务。从委员会的敌对反映我们可以看出,人们对他们是否阻止这篇报道的发表十分好奇这也是合情合理的。通过媒体我们可以看出他们的反对行为企图污蔑人的个性压制人们讨论自由的权利。看起来个性和发言权始终结合在一起。委员会试图阻止人们发言但似乎持不同观点的人以及有怪癖的人会反对这一行为。

239    这个故事会有个好的结局吗?揭发者重新被任用,但似乎并没有在做他的本职工作:

　　　　他重新回到委员会,但被安排到会计部门工作,每天处理一些毫无争议家具订单。

　　　　　　　　　　　　　　《卫报》,1999 年 10 月 13 日

240    他曾写过一本书,但委员会禁止这本书的出版。这是此事进一步发展吗?惩罚有个性的人,限制他们表达自己的思想。当局机关总是能找到很多理由,至少可以禁止书的出版:

　　　　委员会并不打算抑制言论自由,但是那些辩论的主要对象们,他们的公民权利应该受到保护。

　　　　　　　　　　　　　　《卫报》,1999 年 10 月 13 日

难道万·布依特南的书有碍审判的公平性和对那些因 241
受贿被起诉的人的评价带有偏见？如果那样，我们可以根
据"是否伤害他人"来做检举。但是这是真的动机吗？法庭
会支持揭发者吗？

密尔认为在这件事情上，只看是否伤害其他人就来检 242
举还远远不够：

……我们绝不可假定，由于对他人利益的
伤害或者可能伤害这一点单独就能构成社会干
涉的正当理由，所以没有什么时候不能把这种干涉解释成为
正当。

即便万·布依特南的书损害了某些人的利益，这也不 243
是禁止其出版的原因。这虽然只是一种"可能伤害"。但却
再一次证明了社会的价值观最终能战胜其他，让人们听到
被忽略的事件的真相，即便他表达得有点激烈。

在《自传》中，密尔提醒我们《论自由》是一本写给未来 244
的书，我们即密尔所说的未来人类，我们仍然需要他的
理论。

# Mill's On Liberty

## 密尔与《论自由》

# Introduction: Reading *On Liberty* Now

## MILL—THE MOST REASONABLE EXTREMIST

### ' Surely nobody can disagree...?'

Think of your strongest moral belief: what action is most definitely right or most emphatically wrong? Think of the clearest example of a good person, or the most definitive instance of a wicked political policy. Now try to argue against yourself. What is wrong with your moral belief? What could be said against that good person? How would someone defend that political policy?

According to the Victorian philosopher of freedom, John Stuart Mill, if you cannot think of strong counter-arguments, then you do not really understand your own beliefs. Here is one of the many classic statements from his *On*

*Liberty*, the most important defence of freedom of thought, discussion and action in the English language:

> **QUOTATION**
>
> *He who knows only his side of the case knows little of that.*

III   If you cannot imagine what an opponent would say, a real opponent, with serious arguments and reasons, then you do not really know *why* you hold your own opinions or values. Normally, we assume that we need to know the reasons *for* our own views. Asked to explain my strongest belief, I start trotting out the positive reasons in its defence. But Mill thinks we don't truly understand the basis for our most cherished ideas and judgements — not unless we can see the objections. These strong beliefs are precisely the ones on which we have trouble imagining the other side.

IV   Mill is uncompromising and provocative. If a person cannot come up with plausible objections to his dearest beliefs of values, then he does not really have any basis for holding them:

> **QUOTATION**
>
> *His reasons may be good, and no one may have been able to refute them. But if he is equally unable to refute the reasons on the other side, if he does not so much as know what they are, he has no ground for preferring either opinion.*

Mill moves carefully from point to point. This writing is tight-    V
ly reasoned. But in his own way, Mill is a natural extremist.
*On Liberty* is a great work of **reasonable extremism**:

> Mill's Reasonable Extremism: The Method of Arguing
>
> ***Never stop short, if the argument can be taken further.***

In this key passage, Mill insists that if a person does not    VI
know both sides of an issue, ' he has **no ground**' for choosing one side over the other. The' no' is emphatic and total, typical of what makes *On Liberty* **the most provocative statement on liberal principles in the history of
philosophy and political theory**. Every case has two
sides, or many sides. If you only know one, then your opinions are entirely arbitrary. You are choosing your beliefs at
random. Do your strongest beliefs meet this challenge? Are
you sure?

**How can they?**

Now think of the most offensive person in the world. Every-    VII
thing about them is disgusting; they hold every view you
despise. Their lifestyle is truly repugnant to you. Whenever
he or she speaks, their views are despicable and their
words degrade everything that you find valuable. You are
outraged by this person's whole existencc. According to
Mill, your outrage is your own problem. You can try to persuade such a person to change their ways, if you can bear

to talk to them. But that is all. You have no grounds for being protcot"I from the pain of your own disgust or outrage:

> **QUOTATION**
>
> There are many who consider as an injury to themselves any
> conduct which they have a distaste for, and resent it as an
> outrage to their feelings.

VIII  Beyond your effort at reasoning with theis objectionable
person, you are not entitled to campaign against this disgusting lifestyle, or to try to get it prohibited. But Mill believes many social restrictions typify this way of thinking:
people think society should protect them against the existence of lifestyles that offend them:

> **QUOTATION**
>
> In its interferences with personal conduct it [the public] is sel-
> dom thinking of anything but the enormity of acting or thinking
> differently from itself.

IX  Mill insists that others should be absolutely free to offend
us, to live the most offensive lifestyles we can imagine. This
was written in 1895, when Queen Victoria was sovereign of
the British Empire, but the argument still bites, as we enter
the third millennium.

X  Whatever our dearest value, we need people to denounce
and deny it! We need other people to live unacceptable
lives, to make unacceptable choices. Mill's *On Liberty* is

mainly an attempt to explain *why* we need the others, the dissidents and blasphemers, the misfits and nonconform- ists, the awkward squads of all kinds.

# MILL'S LIBERAL VISION

## Stay calm if there's no harm

Liberalism means many different things: a political move- XI ment, a theory set of values, an approach to life. There have been many liberal thinkers, and they have often disa- greed—perhaps that is part of what makes them liberals! But at the centre ofany liberalism is the concept of free- dom. Liberal politics is you the politics of freedom; liberal ethics is you the ethics that starts and finishes with free- dom.

Mill's *On Liberty* is one of the great liberal texts because XII of the argument we have begun to observe—the argument about the individual and society. Like all liberals, Mill faces a problem: surely there must be limits to this liberty? Ac- cording to Mill, there is only one reason for preventing a lif- estyle, or suppressing a view:

> **QUOTATION**
>
> ...the only purpose for which power can rightfully be exer- cised over any member of a civilised community, against his will, is to prevent harm to others.

XIII  If it isn't doing anyone any harm then it cannot legitimately be stopped. Lots of questions arise here, and we will be discussing them later. But one thing is dear: your sensc of outrage does not count as to this liberal vision, can claim to be harmed by views that disgust them, or lifestyles that annoy them. On the contrary, "We will see, Mill insists that offensive lives and alien view are probably necessary: they are doing you good. Society, argyes this most reasonable extremist, needs blasphemers. This make Mill's *On Liberty* one of the texts which pushes liberal thinkinl to the edge.

XIV  Mill's liberal vision allows only that one limit, that of 'harm to others'. There is bound to be an argument about this harm: but one thing is clear, having your feelings hurt, or your ideals besmirched, does not count as being harmed. He gives some famous examples of what does and does not count as harm:

---

**KEY PASSAGE**

Is it really doing any harm?

An opinion that corn-dealers are starvers of the poor, or that private property is robbery, ought to be unmolested when simply circulated through the press, but may justly incur punishment when delivered orally to an excited mob assembled before the house of a corn-deale, or when handed about among the same mob in the form of a placard.

No person ought to be punished simply for being drunk; but a soldier or a policeman should be punished for being drunk on duty.

---

Together, these examples define Mill's liberal vision          XV

The first example is about freedom of expression. In 1859,   XVI
most 'respectable' citizens would not have agreed that
people should be free to write articles denouncing private
property as theft. Mill is saying that the argument is only
harmful, if you can show a direct effect of uttering those
words, in that particular situation.

> **Mill's liberal vision: Freedom of expression**
>
> No value orinstitution is si important to sociew that it is entitled
> to protection from being denounced or criticised.

If someone wants to write diatribes against the family, say,   XVII
or against education, or against the police, we ought to let
them. In fact, we probably ought to encourage them, the
more we find their views offensive. Have you no confidence
in your ability to answer back?

The second example is about character and lifestyle. In our   XVIII
time, UK legislation is being proposed to keep those with
´personality disorders´ off our streets. Mill would dissent,
unless someone is actually being hurt.

> **Mill's liberal vision: Freedom to be yourself**
>
> People's vices, if they are vices, are none of your someone is
> being directly hurt.

The drunkenness example offended many Victorians—as   XIX

Mill intended. This was written in the great period of the temperance movement. But just listen to contemporary British politicians talking about 'yob culture', crowds of youths on the streets! Mill insists that society has no justification for stopping anyone getting drunk, unless they are performing a public role—say an airline pilot, in contemporary discussion.

# WHY READ *ON LIBERTY* NOW?

### A different reason

XX We tend to think of reasoning as a dry process and of being ' reasonable' as mainly about calming down. Doesn't a reasonable person tend to take the middle ground, to compromise, to be, in fact, lukewarm? To read Mill's *On Liberty* is to gain a different sense of **what it means to be reasonable**. Mill's book is you a work of passionate reasonableness, of reasonable extremism.

### A liberal vision

XXI The liberal argument of *On Liberty* is still very much alive in the present. These words still grab our attention, seek to persuade us that **we have not understood the basis of a free society**, that we have not gone nearly far enough in our lazy assent to the value of personal liberty. This Victorian thinker's words still accuse us of being half-hearted in our conventional acceptance of the views and lives of others. Have we really understood the implications of living in a free society, where different people truly hold diverse beliefs and live differing lifestyles? We have not yet ' caught up' with Mill' s arguments.

**Cultural history**

In reading On Liberty, we are tracing **the history of our** XXII **own voices** and key words. Mill' s great book plays a major role in promoting a modern language of freedom. His key terms include words which are still central to our debates about liberty: ' diversity' and ' individuality' , ' conformity' and' interference' . He also helps to define major concepts like' public opinion' and' fashion' .

# OUTLINE OF THIS GUIDE

**Chapter 1**    surveys Mill' s life, particularly as seen in his XXIII own classic *Autobiograpy* and looks briefly at his times.

Chapters 2 onwards form a guided reading of *On Liberty*. The focus is as follows:

**Chapter 2**    discusses the basic theory of ' liberty' . There XXIV is an explanation of the liberal heart of *On Liberty*, and of the relationship between Mill' s liberalism and his wider philosophy of' utility' , ( *On Liberty*, ' Introductory' ) .

**Chapter 3**    explains the other side of Mill' s basic posi- XXV tion, his account of history as the struggle between liberty and authority. Though Mill is most well known for his hard-

edged principles of freedom, he himself always relates theory to actual history. Indeed Mill's idea of history is integral
to his theory of freedom( *On Liberty,* ' Introductory' ) .

XXVI **Chapters 4 and 5**   explain the main arguments that Mill
offers on ' Freedom of Discussion and Thought' . First we
look at his classic dissection of conventional ideas about
liberty of the press. A contemporary example is employed:
The UK Freedom of Information Act. Second, we examine
how Mill systematically destroys conventional assumptions
about the limits of free expression( *On Liberty,* Ⅱ ) .

XXVII **Chapter 6**   introduces Mill's radical defence of' individuality' and his wider theory of human well-being. The account is presented in terms of key sayings or proverbs of
well-being, vivid formulations that light up Mill's argument
( *On Liberty,* Ⅲ ) .

XXVIII **Chapter 7**   considers Mill's vision of his own society, and
how far that social criticism is still applicable to our day
( *On Liberty,* end of Ⅲ , ' Of Individuality' , Ⅳ ' The Individual
and Society' and Ⅴ ' Applications' ) .

# 1

# Mill's Life Story

In his *Autobiography*, John Stuart Mill wrote a classic lire story, one which has provided a model for many later accounts of personal crisis and recovery. The eminent philosopher, Isaiah Berlin, has called this book '*one of the most moving accounts of a human life*'. In this chapter, we follow Mill's life story, putting the tale in context. This story is related directly to the key concepts of *On Liberty*. At the heart of both works, there is a deep commitment to individuality as the source of human well-being. This story is more than just an external background for *On Liberty*; it is you part of the same world.

## THE EARLY YEARS

John Stuart Mill was born on 20 May 1806 in London. His

father was the influential radical thinker James Mill. In his *Autobiography, Mill gives one of the most famous accounts* of a childhood, certainly of a philosopher's childhood. Interpretations have differed radically but everyone, including Mill, agrees that he had an extraordinary childhood, and that it shaped his later life as a thinker. Essentially, Mill tells us how his father educated him at home from an extremely early age until he went off to work in his father's office at the age of 18. John Stuart Mill did not go to school or university. Instead his father established for him a unique experiment in education. At age three, Mill was learning ancient Greek and arithmetic. Soon he was being taken by his father on walks across the fields and reciting the evidence of his day's reading:

3　I made notes on slips of paper while reading, and from these, in the morning walks, I told the story to him; for the books were chiefly histories, of which I read a great number:
Robertson' histories, Hume, Gibbon.

4　Soon Mill was reading Millar's *Historical View of the English Government*. . . Mosheim's *Ecclesiastical History*, Mc-Crie's *Life of John Knox.* '

5　At the age of eight, Mill began Latin, and this part of his life story is a long list of books in different languages. Several of these childhood texts are directly relevant to *On Liberty*, particularly ancient works of political theory by Plato, Aristotle and Cicero. From the age of 12, Mill was taught logic, on which, in adult life, he became a leading authority.

He was also kept busy reading the proofs of his father's own massive *History of British India*, which came out in 18l8. Mill looked back on this work with admiration:

> Saturated as the book is with the opinions and modes of judgement a democratic radicalism then regarded as extreme.

Mill also draws our attention to missing elements in this education, notably the absence of religion, for which he remains grateful. On the other hand, he does look back on a more damaging absence, the lack of affection. For some readers, notably Mill's friend Carlyle, this is the account of a nightmare childhood. For others, such as the contemporary philosopher Jonathan Riley, the verdict is more mixed, as it seems to have been for Mill himself. Many of his father's political ideas continue to find expression within *On Liberty*, but in other ways, as Isaiah Berlin observes, the book can be seen as a reaction against such an upbringing—given its emphasis upon the well-being of the individual and upon the need for people to find their own way of living and thinking.

6

## PERSONAL CRISIS

Mill's father found a post in the East India Company, which was then responsible for the administration of India. In 1823 he found employment for his son, who remained there for 35 years, rising to a high level, until the responsibility for India passed to the Crown.

7

8    In the early 1820s Mill began a phase of active involve-
     ment in the radical political and intellectual circles of the
     time. In the winter of 1822-3 he set up a debating society
     dedicated to the ideas of utilitarianism, the philosophy es-
     poused by his father and by the leading figure, Jeremy
     Bentham, who was a friend of the Mill family. We will be
     considering' utility' as a key element of the arguments of
     *On Liberty*. The classic account of' utility' was provided by
     Bentham hilllself:

9    An action then may be said to be comfortable to the princi-
     ple of utility. . . when the tendency it has to augment
     the happiness of the community is greater than any it
     has to diminish it.

     An Introduction to the Principles of Morals and Legislation

10   The famous shorthand for' utility' was' the greatest happi-
     ness of the greatest number' , a phrase originally used by
     the eighteenth-century radical Joseph Priestley and taken
     over by Bentham. These were the ideas that lay behind the
     development of utilitarianism, which was the philosophy
     with which Mill remained engaged throughout his life,
     though in an increasingly subtle and critical way. In 1823,
     Mill was involved in the start-up of the radical journ *The
     Westminster Review*. In 1824-5, he was busy editing Ben-
     tham's papers on law. Between 1825 and 1830 Mill was a
     leading speaker on behalf of the ideas of The Utilitarian
     Society.

11   However, at the same time, Mill touchingly records that he

experienced a period of deep personal crisis from 1826. It is the honest and authentic account of this personal crisis that has made his *Autobiography* a classic of literature and not merely a background to the philosophy. This is a startlingly modern story of a psychological breakdown and the long road to recovery.

The crisis story is also directly relevant in several different 12 ways to the understanding of *On Liberty*. Mill starts by saying that in the autumn of 1826, he' *was in a dull state of nerves.* ' Soon, he was overtaken by the experience of emptiness, his own life seemed without purpose or value. In this' *dry heavy dejection*' , he felt alone. In particular, he knew he could never approach his dominating father with such feelings. The recovery was also an intellectual revolution. In this story, Mill tells us of his growing recognition of ' *the necessities of human well-being.* ' We shall see that well-being is a central subject in *On Liberty*, and the topic on which Mill continued to speak to the future in important ways. Above all, influenced especially by the poetry of Wordsworth, Mill grasped for the first time, the value of' the internal culture of the individual' .

From 1829, Mill did not attend the debating society. He de- 13 clared that he left behind the old' *system of political philosophy*' and replaced it with ' *a conviction that the true system was something much more complex and many-sided*' . It is this ideal that found expression in *On Liberty*— where many-sidedness is both the content and the approach taken. His ideas were now open to a wider range of infuences, including Carlyle, personally and as a writer, and Coleridge, as well as German philosophy. Mill remained a radical and a supporter of the 1830 French Revolution, but he no longer shared what now seemed his father's uncritical support for democracy as the answer to everything.

14   In 1830 Mill met Harriet Taylor, the love of his life. She was married with children but Harriet became his close friend and, after her husband's death in 1849, they married, in 1851. Her death from tuberculosis occurred shortly before the completion and publication of the great book *On Liberty*, which was dedicated to her memory. Indeed Mill credits Harriet with effectively being the joint author of this and a number of other works.

# WRITINGS

15   John Stuart Mill was an immensely prolific writer, contributing a huge number of articles to different journals. He also wrote a nummber of works which had an immediate influence at the time, and continue to be important today:

16   Influential works

   o In the spring of 1843, he published the great System of *Logic*, defending the view' *which derives all knowledge from experience'*. This remains a major text in the development of modern logic.

   o In 1848, he published *Principles of Political Economy,*

an immediately influential radical view of the economy.

○ In 1854, he wrote a short version of the idea that became *On Liberty*. In 1855 he began to turn it into a book.

In the *Autobiography*, he puts stress on this project being   17 a joint work with Harriet. In his view, ' *The Liberty is likely to survive longer than anything else that I have written*' . He sees it as' *a kind of philosophic text-book of a single truth*' and a declaration of' *the importance, to man and soclety, of a large variety in types of character, and of giving full freedom to human nature to expand itself in innumerable and conflicting directions*' .

There was also a dark side to Mill' s view of the value of   18 *On Liberty*. In the future, he believed, society may become more oppressive of the individual and' *It is then that the teachings of the* Liberty *will have their greatest value.* '

This is a philosophy for the future. It was also a book which   19 had an immediate impact when It appeared in 1859, the year Darwin' s *Origin of Species* was also published. Though contemporaries were hostile to many of Mill' s arguments, notably his critique of their own time, the sheer attention paid to it initiated a phase when Mill became almost a dominating influence. In 1865 he became an MP, campaigning for women' s suffrage, and his writings continued, including the great *Autobiography*, which was published in the year of his death, 1873.

# Liberty in Theory

20    This is the first of two chapters explaining the basics of Mill's arguments as he presents them in the classic 'Introductory' section of *On Liberty*. Mill uses this opening in two ways. First, he sets out his vision in 'Theory' and second, he puts his whole argument in historical perspective. In this chapte, we will examine the theoretical basis of *On Liberty*; the next chapter looks at Mill's view of the history of liberty.

## PROLOGUE TO A THEORY:
## DEFINING 'LIBERTY'

21    Mill starts by defining the 'liberty' with which he is concerned:

> **KEY QUOTE**
>
> Civil or Social liberty: the nature and limits of the power which can legitimately be exercised by society over the individual.

## Anatomy of the Key Quote

○ ' *Civil or Social*' : Mill is not concerned with human free will under God, say, or freedom and fate. His ' liberty' is part of the way human beings exist together, as groups, as societies. It is also worth noting that he does not refer to' political' liberty, for reasons we will soon see. 22

○ ' *power*' : Mill typically thinks in negatives. So he approaches ' liberty' by bringing in' power'. Liberty is defined as the limitation placed upon the exercise of power.

○ ' *legitimately*' : From the start, this argument is about value judgements. Mill wants to make us think about society as a whole. For him, liberty defines a legitimate society. If a society exercises power in ways that overstep the bounds set by liberty, then that society fails Mill's Liberal Legitimacy Test which we will be discussing late. This is probably the most influential outcome of Mill's argument.

○ ' *society*' and ' *the individual*' : This is another antithesis, like liberty and power. The sphere of individuality is defined by the limits of social intervention.

In this key quote, we see Mill thinking in opposites. He un- 23 derstands the meaning of each of the concepts in terms of its opposite but Mill has a particular approach to these oppositions, these binary poles. He approaches them dynamically. He does not establish fixed definitions: this is what society means, that is what the individual means. Instead, Mill is interested in the changing impacts of each concept on the othe. If we look at society in this way, then what effect does that have on our view of the individual?In other words, his approach is **dialectical.** He thinks in moving oppositions.

24　In following through from this key passage, Mill declares that this problem of **liberty** is' *a question seldom stated'* . His aim, he implies, is precisely to state, with new clarity, the liberty question.

**Mill's aims**

25　＊ Mill aims to express the question of liberty in a new way. His view is that this' question' has not even received proper discussion.

＊ Language is important to Mill. He wants to make it possible to state what has previously been unstated.

＊ His widest aim is to achieve an advance in the language of political and moral debate.

26　This unstated question, liberty, is, according to Mill, latent in many other disputes. Here we have a definition of the task of philosophy: to state clearly the question which lies behind public conflict and debate or controversies. It seems possible that the larger aim is to make new agreement possible.

The philosopher reveals the question that is the source of 27 disturbances in the society. All kinds of issues are difficult to resolve, until this underlying question becomes clear.

# MILL'S LIBERAL LEGITIMACY TEST

Mill is not concerned to state the question of liberty purely 28 as an intellectual exercise. In restating liberty, he is also proposing a new standard to be applied in debates about the individual and society.

Liberalism is often assumed to have a wishy-washy out- 29 look, appealing in its openness but also unable to take a clear line. Liberals are seen as easy relativists, settling for splitting the difference between differing views. It is true that Mill often argues from the principle that the human viewpoint is inherently limited. that we live our lives in perspectives that aren't absolute, and that what you see depends on who and where you are. We see the world according to our point of view. Mill is not a relativist when it comes to evaluating a society. Here he thinks he has come up with a **standard test of the legitimacy of any society,** a test provided by his doctrine of liberty.

We have seen Mill defining liberty as the concept that fixes 30 the legitimate uses of power in and by a society. From this follows, as we will see, a wider approach to judging both policies and societies as a whole:

---

**Mill's Liberal Legitimacy Test**

Any society that fails to honour the liberty of the individual is illegitimate. Its use of power cannot be justified if it trespasses on the rightful sphere of individuality.

---

31  This legitimacy test is liberal in that it starts from the question of freedom. An alternative legitimacy test, for example, might be based on a criterion of equality – that a legitimate society must achieve as much equality as possible.

32  Now we need to look at the way Mill develops his idea of liberty into this basis for social judgement. Having defined the term liberty in opposition to power, Mill then offers his principle for testing any given use of authority, any intervention by society into the life of the individual:

---

**KEY QUOTE**

The object of this Essay is to assert one very simple principle, as entitled to govern absolutely the dealings of society with the individual in the way of compulison and control.

---

### Anatomy of the Key Quote

33  ○ '*principle*' : First, the object of the essay is to assert a principle. This raises the issue of what counts as a principle in general. When is an idea or argument also a principle? That turns out to be a very difficult and central

question in the interpretation of Mill, and also then, in, the history of political theory.

For Mill, a principle is a proposition that supplies us with the key to a way of thinking about particular issues. To be a principle, this proposition must apply across the board. On the other hand, a principle is not an automatic solution to any specific issue. Principles need to be applied. They are not the same as rules, as John Gray shows in his influential rereading of *On Liberty*. What makes Mill's essay radical is that he claims to have discovered the principle for deciding when a society is exercising its power legitimately and when, by contrast, it has overstepped the mark. This is an absolutely huge claim. Principles are rare. There are never going to be many coherent principles. In fact, Mill might well argue that our society at present lacks any clear sense of fundamental principles altogether.

○ '*one very simple principle*': Principles are ways of thinking consistently. The aim is to show how we need only 'one principle' as the basis for our thinking about many different issues.

○ '*compulsion and control*': This principle applies both to legal penalties and to the moral coercion of public opinion. Early critics, like James Stephen, objected violently to this constraint on moral pressure: these were, after all, Victorian times! In other words, Mill is interested in the law, but he is also concerned with the general climate.

He wants to know where the law should intervene on, say, drug-taking or fox-hunting. But he also wants to specify the point beyond which society should cease to exert moral pressure in more general ways.

Mill wants us to be consistent across politics and civil society. He will not accept the idea of substituting intense moral pressure for legal sanctions. They are not identical, and we can look at them differently. The case for legal sanctions must be more difficult to make and defend in the end, but still, Mill isn't going to allow a society to replace draconian laws with moral blackmail.

34 Mill then moves on to the most famous formulation in the book:

> **KEY QUOTE**
>
> That principle is, that the sole end for which mankind are warranted, individually or collectively in, interfering with the liberty of action of any of their number is self-protection... the only purpose yor which power can be rightfully exercised over any member of a civilised community, against his will, is to prevent harm to others.

### Anatomy of the Key Quote

35 ○ '*self-protection*' : There is a positive version of the principle of self-protection, which actually comes before the more famous negative version: '*to prevent harm to others*' . To make sense of this pairing, you have to see the

' self' in self-protection as referring to society as a whole, rather than individuals. This is not a theory of justified self-defence; it is about the extent to which a society can limit the action of individuals.

○ ' *mankind*' : A principle is universal, if it is truly a principle. This is what makes Mill' s argument both exciting and alien. We are not used to such criteria. We have all sorts of beliefs, which we think of as generally valid: people should not be cruel, say, or kindness is better than intimidation; but we don' t quite make the leap that Mill demands of his argument here. He is insisting that this principle applies to mankind as a whole, across all of time and space, throughout history.

○ ' *civilised community*' : There is one implied exception: ' *any member of a civilised community*' : The principle is universal but there are places where it does not make sense to apply it, and that is where a society is, in Mill' s terms, not( yet) civilized. In an uncivilized state, Mill concedes, it will be necessary at times to limit individual action more rigorously than in a civilized state. When you think about the context, you can see that this turns out be a controversial assumption. This book was written at the height of the British Empire, by a man with a career in Indian administration. Mill was certainly a' progressive' in his attitude to the empire but his argument still implies a rigid distinction between people who count as civilized and others. This approach has struck some later commentators, notably Gray, as too rigid for our times.

36    Any society that uses power differently violates legitimate limits. At the centre of Mill's theory of liberty is his' Harm Criterion'. If you cannot show that an act will harm someone, then you are not entitled to prevent that act – either by law or by social pressure.

---

**Liberal Legitimacy Test: The Harm Criterion**

There is only one ground for restricting individuals, and that is when what they are doing will harm other people. A society is legitimate if it exercises power within those limits. Any other exercise of power is illegitimate.

---

37    A society violates human liberty if acts are prevented beyond the Harm Criterion. This is a big idea and certain questions arise immediately. As critics from Hutton in 1859 onwards have wondered, what exactly counts as harm? Clearly physical injury is harmful but you can't say a society is entitled only to regulate its members by preventing them physically attacking one another! Fraud, forgery, and robbery of all kinds, deception, some lies: a long list of other kinds of harm unfolds immediately. Then there is the more difficult area. What about emotional and psychological damage? Is hurting someone's feelings doing him or her harm? And who gets to decide if someone's feelings are legitimately hurt by an act, or by an utterance?

38    How far is this principle meant to go? It seems to tell us how to set certain limits but you wouldn't be able to use

this principle to decide what was a good law, say; only to decide what was a legitimate law, and what was a law too far.

## Mill's Liberal Legitimacy Test: An example

Drugs and hunting are two issues on which there is wide-   39
spread debate and division. They are the issues of our time. In each case, the question can be put in Mill's terms: What is the extent of ' *the power which can legiti-mately be exercised by society over the individual'* . In the case of drugs, the problem is how far society has a duty to protect individuals from themselves. In the case of hunting, the issue is how far the disapproval of one section of society can or should be legally enforeed over another.

Mill does not offer a simple way to resolve such disputes   40
but his theory provides a way of getting the issues clear. Let's take two people:

Jake, an 18-year-old student, is strongly in favour of a ban   41
on fox-hunting. He believes that this activity violates animal rights and he wants this outrage expressed in law. He also thinks that soft drugs should be legalized, that it is a viola-tion of the rights of the individual to be told that he cannot explore the experience of say Ecstasy, or cannabis. Why should whisky be legal, when dope isn't?

Margaret, a 43-year-old mother and rural shopkeeper, is   42
strongly opposed to the fox-hunting ban. She thinks it is outrageous interference by strangers in the life of her com-

munity. She is also strongly against the legalization of drugs and thinks that there needs to be a strong campaign to enforce the law on such matters.

43　Mill does not want us to leap to one side or the other on such issues. He wants us:

* First, to identify the underlying question: liberty, the extent of the legitimate power of society over individuals.

* Second, to apply' one. . . principle' to all such' controversies' .

44　For both Jake and Margaret, the two controversies, fox-hunting and drug legalization, are entirely separate matters. This is what Mill denies and, in doing so, he challenges the entire nature of all our opinions and judgements. From Mill' s point of view, our judgements are *unprincipled*. We have beliefs and opinions, but we never subject these beliefs to the *test of principle*. Are we thinking consistently?Do the opinions that we have about, say, hunting bans fit with our views about drug legalization?I think the answer is often that we are effectively unprincipled in our beliefs. It is not just individuals who are unprincipled either – politics is, in this sense, unprincipled. We often hear about politicians lacking principles in a different sense. What this usually means is that they are not scrupulous enough about taking favours. But Mill' s essay suggests that our whole political sphere is devoid of principle. Political parties take up positions on individual issues without any clear sense of whether those positions have a consistent basis.

# BEYOND LIBERTY?

In setting out the basics of his theory, Mill immediately     45
faces a wider problem. How many other principles are we
going to need?And how are those other principles going to
relate to this' one simple principle' of liberty and its use in
practice to determine the legitimacy of the uses of power.
In two important ways, Mill does look' beyond liberty' .

### The Rationality Criterion

First, there is a criterion that limits the whole application of     46
liberty. We have already touched on this, but Mill now
faces it squarely:

> **KEY QUOTE**
>
> Liberty, as a principle, has no application to any state of
> things anterior to the time when mankind have become capa-
> ble of being improved by free and equal discussion.

### Anatomy of the Key Ouote

○ ' *capable*' : In effect, Mill has defined civilization here. A     47
civilized state is one where people have become capa-
ble of certain relationships to one another and to their society.

- ' *improved*' : This is a dangerous term for Mill to have in-
  voked. We will see him objecting to the desire to improve
  others. But here he means that civilized people will improve without compulsion – freely.

- ' *free and equal discussion*' : In a civilized state, individuals have become capable of responding to the reasoning
  of others. This is a strong idea, and it goes way beyond
  liberty itself.

48  Alongside his famous Harm Criterion, then, Mill adds this
Rationality Criterion. In Mill' s argument, this Rationality Criterion comes before the Liberal Legitimacy Test. You have
to show that a society meets the Rationality Criterion before
you are entitled to apply a liberty test at all. In a pre-civi-
lized society, all kinds of interence with the individual may
be legitimate. This means that liberty cannot be Mill' s sole
value, or even his main value. He must have other axes to
grind.

**The ultimate appeal: utility**

49  Mill is one of the founding thinkers of modern liberalism,
and his liberty principle belongs in the tradition of liberal
thought. However, as we saw in the last chapter, he also
belongs to the philosophical school known as ' Utilitarianism' , one of the most influential approaches of nineteenth
and twentieth-century philosophy. At the same time as he
wrote *On Liberty*, Mill also wrote his definitive work on this
' Utilitarianis' , defining the basis of that wider approach to

life.

We have seen that the key concept in utilitarian thought is    50
not liberty, but utility. Critics have accused Mill of failing to
deal coherently with the relationship of utility to liberty. By
utility is meant the happiness-producing or pain-reducing
power of any act or decision or state of affairs. According
to utilitarian thought, we must refer to such utility in making
our choices. We should choose the option that has the
great utility, which means producing the most pleasure or
the least pain. This does not mean just for me; it means for
everyone affected – so it is not simply a selfish approach.
Mill immediately connects this view of utility to his argument about liberty:

---

**KEY QUOTE**

I regard utility as the ultimate appeal on all ethical questions;
but it must be utility grounded on the permanent interests of
many as a progressive being.

---

## Anatomy of the Key Quote

○ ' *ultimate*' : When it comes to practical decision-making,    51
  what takes precedence is utility. You choose on the basis
  of the happiness-inducing, or pain-reducing, effects of
  your choice.

○ ' *permanent interests*' : Both words are critical. Mill is not
  talking about transient effects, the passing pleasure of
  one person; he is concerned with lasting consequences,

benefits and costs that do not fade with their context. This question of how interests are defined has been much discussed, notably by Berlin.

- ○ '*man as a progressive being*' : Authentic utility is what would make a rational person happy – or what would contribute to the growing happiness of the human race as a maturing entity though history.

52 We now have the outlines of Mill's approach — and the most important point is that he has several ideas, not one. Though this book is about one major question, the individual and society, Mill is definitely not the kind of thinker who believes he can stick to one single idea.

53 At the centre of the argument about liberty is the Liberal Legitimacy Test with the Harm Criterion: no harm equals no restriction.

54 But in two key ways Mill also needs to look beyond liberty:

1 The Rationality Criterion: no civilized reasoning means no question of liberty.

2 The ultimate appeal – utility: always choose in the interests of human happiness in the largest sense.

55 Mill's real problem is how these ideas relate to each other. This is not just a personal problem, it is the key difficulty which liberal theory has to overcome. Individual liberty is necessary, but not sufficient to define a good society, or a right policy or use of power.

For some critics, Mill does not give a definite enough an- 56
swer to the problem of reconciling liberty with rationality
and utility. He is sometimes seen as being a utilitarian in
liberal clothing – smuggling a utility dogma in under the
pretence of defending individual freedom. Others accuse
him of shuffling from one concept to another when it suits
his argument.

Two points may be made in Mill's defence: 57

1 Mill is a dialectical thinker. He does not offer a rule or a
   system, he proposes concepts that we have to balance
   against each other This process of balancing is dialectical, in the sense that we are weighing different forces,
   pulling in contrary directions. Mill aims to start a
   process, not give a solution.

2 The liberty principle is *not* Mill's ultimate 'test for specific choices or policies. This is important' because it dis-
   tinguishes Mill from many other thinkers and a great deal
   of modern politicians. No one has been more serious a-
   bout freedom than Mill – but he does not have the illusion
   that the first person to refer to freedom in an argument
   will be on the winning side. Yet that is pretty much how a
   lot of modern political and cultural debate has worked.

# 3

# Liberty in History

58　We have seen how Mill proposes a theory of freedom and how that theory has been hugely influential. But in fact, there is another side to Mill' s view of freedom – an historical dimension. In this chapter, we explore Mill' s version of human history as the evolution of liberty. Without this history, the theory hangs in a vacuum. Mill is not really the kind of thinker who works in abstract formulae. He seeks always to connect his principles with actual societies and real histories, as he understands them. In fact, *On Liberty* is at least as much a vision of history as it is an argument about values.

## THE PROGRESSIVE BEING OF HUMANITY

59　In the previous chapter, we saw how Mill defined his principle of utility as referring to the lasting benefit of' *man as a progressive being*' . History is the field where this' progressive being' finds expression but there is nothing complacent or simple about Mill' s version of historical progress.

For Mill, as for Marx, history does not mean the past or    60
past events. Both thinkers see the present as a phase in a process that connects all that has been with the possible future. In other words, history is a living process, which includes his own age:

---

**KEY QUOTE**

... the stage of progress into which the more civilised portions of the species have now entered.

---

### Anatomy of the Key Quote

○ ' *stage*' : We tend to talk in terms of historical' periods' ,    61
neutral and directionless slices of time. By comparison, for Mill, a' stage' suggests an unfolding trajectory. This is an approach also found in Marx, in Hegel and in Comte. There is an analogy implied between historical progress and individual growth. It is as if there was a natural progression from less advanced stage to more advanced.

○ ' *civilised portions*' : Mill' s arguments involve a strong sense of the one-ness of humanity. Though some parts are, in his terms, more civilized, they still belong to the whole. We have seen that civilized for Mill, refers not to

moral or technological development, but to ' free and e-
qual discussion ' .

○ ' *species* ' : As we saw, Mill' s *On Liberty* was published
in 1859, the same year as Darwin' s *Origin of Species*.
Behind the logic of human history, there is the pattern of
natural history.

62 It always seems to us that Victorian ideas of progress are
complacent. Why should one assume that history was naturally moving forwards? The crises of the twentieth century
seem to have undermined this assumption of a trajectory
through time, but there is, in fact, another way of holding a
belief in progress. Far from being complacent about the
present, Mill uses the idea of progress to challenge his
own time. The present itself is simply a stage. There will be
a future from whose point ofview this moment will be as
limited as the dark ages now seem to the Victorians era.

63 The first feature of history is progress – but the second feature is struggle:

---

**KEY QUOTE**

The struggle between Liberty and Authority is the most con-
spicuous feature in the portions of history with which we are
earliest familiar.

---

## Anatomy of the Key Quote

64 ○ ' *earliest* ' : Where does history start? What is the first
scene of the drama? For Mill, history begins as ' strug-

gle'. No doubt, there are phases before struggle, but they do not merit the title of history at all. What counts as historical time is defined by conflict. History is the story of a fundamental antithesis, and society comes into existence as the medium through which certain oppositions fight for supremacy.

○ '*struggle*' : This idea of history as' struggle' is central to the philosophy of Hegel, the dominant influence on nineteenth-century philosophy of history. In his thought, oppositions drive history forwards betweeen ideas.

1 Marx takes over Hegel's approach to history as' struggle.' In the 1848 *Communist Manifesto*, history is a series of stages in the class struggle.

2 The term for this view of history is' dialectical'.

In Hegel, the dialectic was a struggle between ideas. In Marx, dialectic was the conflict between social forces, called classes. The nineteenth century was the phase of the conflict between the bourgeois class and the working class. Mill has his own version of the dialectic, as the unfolding of the conflict between freedom and its antitheses at different stages of human and social develooment.

## THE DIALECTIC OF LIBERTY

In the previous chapter, we saw how Mill defined a liberty　65 principle in universal terms: liberty is the criterion by which we decide on the legitimate relations between society and the individual. But now we see his other perspective. Liberty has a history, in which it means different things as it encounters changing counterforces.

> **Mill's Dialectic of Liberty**
>
> Human history expresses the the struggle between two principles: liberty and authority.

66  Mill surveys history, as 'we' know it: Greece, Rome and England. There is, as Gray emphasizes, something surprisingly unquestioning about Mill's assumptions that history belongs in the West, and that it begins in classical Greece particularly. There is also something oddly naïve about the way he attaches England to classical Greece and Rome. This is more Victorian mythology than history in a modern sense. On the other hand, within that limitation, Mill has an interesting view of the shape of history.

**The first stage: the tyrannical era**

67  In the first stage, liberty comes into being as the opposite of **tyranny:**

> **QUOTATION**
>
> By liberty, was meant protection against the tyranny of the political rulers.

Mill's history starts as total oppression:                               48

> **Mill's Dialiectic of Liberty**
>
> First stage: The Era of Original tyranny
>
> In the time of the tyrants, Liberty is the people's shield against absolute rule.

During the first stage the rulers believe they can do as they    69
please; they think of their subjects as mere objects to be
used at will. Mill defines this original society as 'political tyranny'. Politics begins as tyranny, not as freedom. Liberty
is born as the enemy of this version of politics.

> **Definition: 'political'**
>
> 'The political' starts as pure power; liberty begills as the alter-native to 'political power'.

In the first stage of history, the tyrannical era, politics is    70
born to express the will of the rulers. Everything else is outside the political sphere. This is important because it
means that liberty does not begin as a political principle,
but rather as the opposite of 'the political'. Liberty is the
counter-value to the will of the rulers:

> **QUOTATION**
>
> The rulers were conceived... as a necessarily antago – nistic position to the people whom they ruled.

71    Greek democracy is seen as an early exception – a sign of things to come. But in the main, the first phase has a clear meaning: rulers against ruled.

72    In the first phase, liberty emerges as the **principle of society**, to set against the rule of politics. The rulers begin politics; liberty is begun by the ruled. Therefore, Mill does not see liberty as a political principle but rather as a social principle, defined in opposition to the realm of political power. The state is not the natural source of liberty, but rather its original enemy. Liberty is born outside politics.

> **Definition: Original liberty**
>
> Liberty is created by society in the face of political power.

73    Liberty is the concept that the ruled develop to resist political tyranny. In dialectical terms, it is tyranny that gives birth to liberty.

74    The whold of Mill's approach is implicit in this starting-point. This original concept of liberty is a negative idea, a reaction against tyranny. Famously, Rousseau declared that man was born free: that can be called romantic liberty. For Mill, as for Marx, liberty is born out of social resistance to oppression. Freedom is not the original state of individuals. On the contrary, freedom is born in the struggle of society to resist the absolute will of the original tyrants. This is important because Mill is traditionally criticized for being too much of an individualist Here we can see that, in fact, Mill conceives of liberty itself as a *social* creation.

## The second stage: the birth of democracy

Each stage of history is defined by its own concept of lib-    75
erty. In the first phase, liberty means the 'limitation' of the
absolute power of the political rulers. The second stage
begins when the people begin to enter the political
sphere. Now liberty loses its previous meaning. In the
second stage, a new struggle begins:

> **QUOTATION**
>
> As the struggle proceeded for making the ruling power ema-
> nate from the periodical choice of the ruled.

Now the struggle is no longer between active tyrants and    76
resisting subjects. Instead, the people develop a positive
aim: to make the rulers into vehicles of their will. This second phase is the birth of democratic society and its key e-
vent is the French Revolution.

> **Mill's Dialectic of Liberty**
>
> Second stage: The Birth of Democracy
>
> The democratic spirit seeks to seize power for society. Liberty
> is no longer the shield of the ruled against the rulers, but part
> of the demand for power.

Since the people aim to take power, they do not need an i-    77
dea of liberty as the defence against that power. Instead,
they assume that once they have power, they will necessa-

rily be free.

---

**KEY QUOTE**

The nation did not need to be protected against its own will.

---

### Anatomy of the Key Quote

78    ○ ' *nation*' : This is the central concept of nineteenth-century politics and history. The birth of democracy is part of the self-expression of the nation, what is still called ' national self-determination'.

○ ' *will*' : There are many versions of the idea of the ' will' in nineteenth-century philosophy. Rousseau based his theory of democracy on an idea of ' the general will' of the people.

---

**Second stage: liberty**

Liberty means access to power, not protection against power.

---

79    When the people are in power, tyranny is surely impossible. If the nation itself is the ruler: ' *There was no fear of its tyrannizing over itself* '.

80    In the first phase, there was a conflict between rulers and ruled, between politics and society. In the second stage, the ruled aspire to become the rulers and society takes command of politics for itself. Politics is reborn as the

process by which society governs itself. In that context, it appears as if the old idea of liberty is redundant.

This is a good example of Mill' s dialectical view of liberty.  81
As society goes through different phases, the meaning of liberty actually changas. There are two sides to this history of liberty. On the one hand, an idea does seem to march through history – the idea of freedom. On the other hand, that idea is interpreted in radically new ways by each new era.

## The third stage: the tyranny of the majority

A third phase is already implied. In this next phase, the  82
rule of the people gives birth to a new kind of tyranny –
' *the tyranny of the majority*' .

In the third stage of this dialectic of liberty, the rule of the  83
people becomes a new tyranny. In fact, of course, there was far from a pure democracy in Mill' s time – he himself campaigned for a widening of the vote, particularly to include women – but by the tyranny of the majority he meant something more than a merely electoral effect:

> **KEY QUOTE**
>
> . . . when society is itself the tyrant – society collectively over the separate individuals who compose it – its means of tyrannizing are not restricted to the acts wich it may do by the hands of its political functionaries.

## Anatomy of the Key Quote

84 ○ '*collectively*' : This is an early example of the negative use of 'collective' in opposition to 'individuals'. In this key passage, we see a paradox of social being. Society is made of individuals; yet the collective takes on its own life, and turns itself into the enemy of each and every 'separate' individual.

○ '*political functionaries*' : This is a satirical term for the elected leaders and representatives in a democratic system. The word 'funtionaries' implies a bureaucratic role. When Mill stood as an MP, he warned the electors that he would not be bound by their wishes!

85 The majority has many ways of imposing its will. Politics is merely one weapon of the majority in its effort to force all minorities to conform. In the third phase, the struggle is between a tyrannical majority and oppressed minorities.

| Mill's Dialectic Of Liberty | Social structure | Power structure |
|---|---|---|
| Phase one | Original society | Absolute rulers against the people |
| Phase two | The democratic upheaval | The people take control of their rulers |
| Phase three | Settled democracy | The tyranny of the majority |

86 The struggle began as a battle between rulers and ruled,

tyrants and peopie. In between there is the birth of **democracy**. Now the struggle is between a dominant majority and excluded minorities, or even every individual as a distinct being. To start with, society was under the thumb of power politics, but now society itself has become the oppressor: ' *society collectively*' . This third phase is the struggle between the collective spirit and the individual, between conformity and difference. The third phase is the era of **social oppression.**

It is clear that Mill thinks his own society has entered this 87 third phase, though it still has some way to go. In effect, this is the era of modern society, or mass society. What does liberty mean now? Liberty must be reborn as the counter-principle not to the absolute rulers, but to the majority:

> **QUOTATION**
>
> There is a limit to the legitimate interference of collective opinion with individual independence.

> **Mill' s Dialectic of Liberty**
>
> Third stage: Settled Democracy
>
> Liberty means the limitation on the tyranny of the majority over minorities, and individuals.

Across history, the meaning of liberty has reversed: this is 88 the dialectic of the idea. To start with, liberty meant the protection of the vast majority against the arbitrary will of the rulers. By this third stage, liberty means the protection of others against the arbitrary will of the majority. The meaning of liberty changes as the nature of tyranny alters. In effect, each new phase of tyranny gives birth to its own corresponding idea of liberty. This is you the essence of Mill' s dialectical view of history.

89   Mill' s own theory of liberty belongs to the third phase, ' the tyranny of the majority' . He has a very dark view indeed of this phase. In previous eras, tyranny was external: brute force, physical violence. It was also possible to fight back through action. But now the tyranny has become internal: it hides and grows inside each person. ' Social tyranny' is worse than' political oppression' , for Mill, because it is so much harder to overcome:

---

**QUOTATION**

. . . it leaves fewer means of escape, penetrating much more deeply into the details of life, and ensalving the soul itself.

---

90   This is the darkest moment in *On Liberty*, a moment of bitter pessimism. This side of the book is often overlooked, the emphasis falling upon the positive philosophy of freedom, and on the formula for applying it to – the Harm Criterion. But Mill also has this dark side to his outlook. He sees progress itself as giving rise to a new and more frightening

kind of oppression.

| Historical stage | Modernity *The third stage* | Traditional The first phase |
|---|---|---|
| Agent of oppression | Social majority | Political tyranny |
| Means of oppression | External force | Interior influence |

In Mill´s view of history, the second stage, the birth of de-   91
mocracy, is the transition between traditional and modern
society. In modern times, people are made into the means
of their own oppression, the majority tyrannizes as much o-
ver its own members as over minorities. In modern times,
nobody is free.

**Towards the fourth stage: conformity or diversity?**

Mill´s own theory of liberty is the counter-idea of the tyr-   92
anny of the majority. His theory is universal but, like Marx´
s theories, also recognizes its own place in history. These
are dangerous times, when progress itself is giving rise to
a new tyranny. Neither have things reached their darkest
point:

> **QUOTATION**
>
> The majority have not yet learnt to feel the power of the gov-
> ernment their power, or its opinions their opinions.

When the majority becomes truly at home with power, then   93 the new tyranny will begin in earnest. Every exception will be an outrage. The law will be made into the vehicle for suppressing differences.

94   As yet, the majority has not understood its new role. People retain some of the attitudes of the earlier phase, when the government acted against the will of the majority. Some of the old instincts of ancient liberty still continue. But over time, the people will understand their new status and then there will be an urgent need for a countervailing doctrine of individual liberty. In the next phase, liberty will become the shield of the minority, and the majority will see liberty as their enemy:

---

**Mill's Dialectic of Liberty**

Towards a fourth stage

In the future, the majority may identify completely with the state; liberty will appear to them as an enemy.

To the minorities, and the individual who recognizes her or his separateness, liberty will then become the principle of difference.

---

95   Unlike Marx, Mill does not see his dialectical view of history as a way to predict the future – but he does hint at different possible futures. Clearly, there is a dark prospect, the fulfilment of the principle of authority under the rule of the majority.

---
**The dark fourth stage: the age of conformity**

---

However, there is also hope. As the dialectic sharpens to    96
its crisis, the concept of liberty reveals its most radical
meaning. In the face of universal **conformism**, liberty will
be the banner of difference:

---
**QUOTATION**

The only freedom which deserves the name is that of pursuing
our own good in our own way.

---

On the horizon, there is also an age of individuality. In that    97
future, liberty would become the ruling idea of society, and
diversity would replace conformity as the social principle.

---
**The bright fourth stage: the age of diversity**

---

The horizon remains open, but there is a utopian possibility    98
implicit in Mill's view of history. Perhaps the struggle will
culminate in an era when the individual is truly flee to pur-
sue his or her own idea of the good life, for better and
worse. In that case, by the dialectic of liberty, the age of
conformity will have given birth to a new phase of diversity.

# Liberty of the Press and Public Interest

99   We now come to the heart of Mill's arguments, Chapter II of *On Liberty*, ' Of the Liberty of Thought and Discussion'. Here he examines **free speech**, one of the most fundamental aspects of modern freedom and one which Mill has most directly influenced. Mill helped to create the agenda of free speech, and his analysis still applies to contemporary controversies where the state, the government, the law or powerful private institutions attempt to constrain public opinion and argument. We will be examining in depth Mill's arguments on freedom of public expression, both in their historical perspective and for their continuing relevance. In this chapter, we focus in close-up on his first case – press freedom – because it is so beautifully argued and so directly relevant.

# STEP ONE: PINNING DOWN THE ACCEPTED VIEW

At the start of' Of the Liberty of Thought and Discussion'. 100
Mill offers for his readers' recognition a would-be principle. He calls it, in the terminology of his age and its predecessors, ' *the liberty of the press*' . Presumably, he declares with apparent confidence, no one needs to spend
any. time nowadays defending or justifying this basic liberty. Everyone accepts that the press must be free, in general, don' t they?But what, he adds, just in case anyone has
forgotten, is really meant by liberty of the press?

Here Mill begins to give **definitions** and, whenever he 101
does so, you know that the argument is about to take a
leap forward – for it is always his aim to unsettle the familiar view of the most important words in public discussion,
and to make space for new meanings to emerge. In effect,
Mill now applies his dialectical understanding of the history
of liberty to a specific case. He is going to show how ' liberty of the press' is an idea from an earlier phase in the
historical dialectic of freedom. Unless rethought for the
new phase, this once valuable idea will become destructive.

First, then, he defines the inherited understanding of liberty 102
of the press: ' " *liberty of the press*" . . . *one of the securities
against corrupt or tyrannical government.* ' In this respect,

it means restraining a government that is not founded upon any democratic or public mandate. No government that is ' *not identified in interest with the people*' shall be entitled to' *determine what doctrines*' they can hear. This concept derives from the first phase in the dialectical history of liberty, the phase of the basic struggle between tyrants and the people as a whole, between pure power and society.

> **STEP ONE**
>
> Liberty of the press: accepted definition
>
> The conventional principle: no power or government shall be entitled to regulate the ideas reaching the public if they do not represent that public.

103 According to Mill, this understanding of press freedom has been passed down to his age by its predecessors. The source of this liberty is really in such events as the Civil War of the seventeenth century, and the religious and political persecutions undertaken by monarchs and their appointed governors. These were the upheavals that brought an end to the first phase of the history of liberty.

104 This is a typical example of Mill's general technique. He wants to show how the words we inherit belong to the ages from which they come. If we continue to use the language of the past – and no other language is *unthinkingly* available to us – we will automatically repeat the arguments of the past. He has already prepared the ground for a fundamental revision of this key sense of liberty as it applies to

public discussion and to ideas. In the current phase of history, the old liberty is out of context. The press no longer needs defending against absolute monarchs.

We are about to begin the journey from the traditional 105 meaning, embodied in the inherited phrase ' liberty of the press' , to the modern meaning, which is represented by Mill' s' liberty of thought and discussion' . This is a concept that belongs to the age of the tyranny of the majority – the third phase of the history we saw in the previous chapter. Now power has passed from the tyrants to the people. The old defensive liberty is you outdated and a new threat is arising – the third phase where the will of the majority becomes the main threat.

With his usual quiet cunning, Mill has opened a trapdoor 106 under the reader who has accepted with a nod the familiar meaning of liberty. Yes, the press should always be free to include whatever opinions it wants – and no government is entitled to intervene if it does not speak on behalf of the public interest. Mill simply leaves the trap quietly in place. However, if you pause over the argument, you can already see much of the logic of the ensuing discussion. What happens when the government *is* more representative? According to Mill, liberty of the press has been developed as a defence against *unrepresentative* governments, absolute kings and other classical tyrannies. Already by the mid-nineteenth century, there are elections. True, the electorate is narrow, and Mill is one of the principal campaigners for a wider electorate. But the Victorians already have passed the age when the government was simply a hostile force at odds with the interests of society. What will this older principle of liberty mean as government becomes ever more representative of the interest and voice of the public?

# STEP TWO: DECONSTRUCTING THE ACCEPTED VIEW

107 Mill begins to turn the phrase 'liberty of the press' round for our consideration. He reassures us – or appears to – that only in cases of exceptional panic would any modern government try to stifle public debate. Unless faced by an imminent revolution, the enlightened authorities of the nineteenth century will not lapse into the style of past despots. Irony is in the air. This is the next stage of a characteristic Mill argument:

---

**STEP TWO**

Traditional 'liberty of the press' : an ironic perspective

In modern times, liberty of the press is assured except in cases of extreme panic or threat to the legitimate order.

---

108 We already have to wonder how far a liberty is real, if a government can choose to revoke it in 'serious' circumstances? Isn't a crisis exactly the moment when public debate is most heated, and most necessary?

Mill now sharpens the irony. The argument enters its sec- 109
ond phase, which one can call the **deconstruction** of the
inherited meaning of ' liberty of the press'. Mill shows up
contradictions within this apparently benign and established word. He is taking us towards a paradox, where the
old doctrine of' liberty of the press' collapses. In a modern
society, the old' liberty' could become a means by which
an elected government can actually justify large-scale and
frequent censorship. Indeed any authority that can claim to
be representative of a public will be able to argue that it
leaves opinion absolutely free, *except* when the interests of
that public require censorship. The dialectic of history has
uprooted the old liberty of the press – it no longer serves to
defend the people against the tyrants. Instead, it threatens
to reinforce the supposed' right' of an elected government
to restrict public discussion.

Little explosions begin to go off in Mill' s apparently peace- 110
ful logic. He reassures us that in constitutional countries,
by which he means those where some degree of public
say is allowed in choosing the government, no authority
' *will often attempt to control the expression of opinion*'.
There is, it seems, a natural link between political democracy and freedom of discussion. That link. surely, is implicit in
the idea that liberty of the press serves the interests of the
public at large.

Of course, Mill adds, in a modern society, a government 111
will never suppress opinions or ideas simply out of its own

tastes or judgements. No modern government would be so arrogant. On the contrary, a constitutional government will suppress opinions only when it is truly confident that it is acting as:

---

**KEY QUOTE**

... the organ of the general intolerance of the public.

---

## Anatomy of the Key Quote

112 ○ '*general intolerance*' : Toleration is the original founding concept of liberal philosophy and practice. Toleration begins as the argument against religious persecution, and becomes a more general approach to differing values and ways of life. The enemy of the liberal, therefore, was religious persecution, and is you now its descendant, the spirit of intolerance. We can see the same antagonism in the very different liberalism of Mill's contemporary, Matthew Arnold.

○ '*the public*' : The whole concept of ' the public' is born with the age of democracy. The public is the collective spirit. The majority acts as the public when seeking to suppress all minorities and eccentrics. The public is a majority that refuses to acknowledge any exceptions.

○ In other words, if liberty of the press means the right to express any view, which *the public wants to hear*, then a government that really represents that public—its interest—will have the right, even the duty, to suppress those views which the public is quite unanimous about not wanting to hear.

The old liberty is inadequate for a changing world. There 113 was a time when it was enough to found liberty of the press upon the right of the public to hear those ideas *which it wished* to hear. That was when the enemy of free discussion was absolute monarchy, acting without regard to the public interest, indeed habitually acting against that public interest. But as government comes under the sway – formally and informally – of public opinion, then this old version of liberty will no longer protect free debate. Now Mill is beginning to set up a contrast between the old version of liberty and his own new Legitimacy Test – that interference is only to be justified on grounds of actual harm.

Mill unfolds a darkening future: **democracy without free-** 114 **dom**. In a democratic age, even a half or quarter democratic age, a new theory of liberty will be necessary. The old principles – freedom for the people – will simply serve to strengthen any authority that represents the public, or society. You can actually *feel* the word liberty slipping loose from past meanings. Mill is a master of this quiet deconstruction: a familiar word softly implodes. In the space, Mill prepares a new meaning of 'liberty' : after the deconstruction, there will be a reconstruction, which carries on for the rest of *On Liberty* – '*the reconstruction of liberty as a restraint on the will of the majority.*'

115 Mill has shown us why traditional doctrines of liberty will not keep a democracy free. Liberty of the press is meant to be the phrase that safeguards the freedom of public discussion, the widest possible communication of ideas and arguments but, Mill shows, the unthinking use of the phrase will have the reverse effect. Liberty of the press could even become the cornerstone of a doctrine of control and limitation, a founding principle of a democratic form of censorship. This will happen if liberty continues to be understood as defined by public interest or opinion, or by the rights of a legitimately representative government.

---

**STEP TWO**

Traditional 'liberty of the press': a deconstruction

No government will be entitled to suppress public discussion of an opinion or idea unless:

∗ that government is acting fully as the 'voice' of the public, or in accordance with public interest;

∗ there is extreme danger to the legitimate order.

---

116 In effect, therefore, we have reached a paradox: the goal of Mill's ironic method of defining accepted terms. The better a government is, in the sense of being representative of public opinion, the worse it might become, in the sense of feeling justified in suppressing unwanted ideas. There is you nothing in the unthinking version of liberty of the press to prevent such a government from suppressing any ideas that annoy its public. It will permit absolute free-

dom except when its' coercion' harmonizes with the public interest and articulates' agreement' with the public' voice'. The old liberty becomes the basis for a new tyranny.

> **Traditional 'liberty of the press': an impossible paradox**
>
> The more closely a government or authority represents the public and voices its opinion, the more entitled it is to suppress the expression of unwanted opinions or ideas.

The same idea of liberty, which was revolutionary in one 117 age, could support oppression in the next. This is the dialectical insight implicit in the critical, or deconstructive phase of Mill's argument, an insight with implications far beyond the specific cases and contexts under discussion in his text.

## MILL IN THE TWENTY-FIRST CENTURY

Mill has now prepared the ground for his wider argument 118 about free speech and thought. Clearly he is going to argue the need for a difierent account of liberty, one that makes it more difficult for modern governments and the public to suppress unpopular views and voices. However, before we follow those arguments, it is worthwhile considering the continuing relevance of his specific analysis of the doctrine of liberty of the press with reference to contemporary relations between government and the media. How does our time fare in relation to Mill's Liberal Legitimacy Test?

119 When you look at the detail, you might think that Mill' s arguments have dated, that he is addressing issues of the mid-nineteenth century. It is certainly important to recognize the degree to which *On Liberty* belongs to its age. Mill is arguing about the prospects for democracy; we are living in the aftermath of those arguments. The time before any meaningful elections at all is still close at hand for Mill, and the memory of the struggle between society and absolute monarchy is still flesh. Nevertheless, his approach is still directly relevant in a number of ways.

# DEMOCRATIC CENSORSHIP IN THE TWENTY-FIRST CENTURY

120 One of the main ways in which a modern government regulates and restricts public debate is through its control of **access to information**. Clearly if information is not available, discussion is limited or impossible. So one of the most powerful means of censorship is the withholding of information – much of which is either directly or indirectly under government control. The government' s authority for controlling this information flow derives directly from its democratic mandate. As our representatwe, the government is entitled to decide where to limit access to information, if there are grounds for thinking it might have a disastrous effect on the public interest. An example might be re-

search on a safety issue, where release of data might cause undue panic, or economic crisis, and where there is still a specialist debate.

Another example might be information about disagree- 121 ments between ministers and officials; or release of data that would help terrorists or military opponents.

In the UK this problem has given rise to a continuing de- 122 bate about **freedom of information**. In 1994, the then Conservative government introduced a code of openness – the central principle being that the grounds for withholding information were primarily based on a' **test of harm**'. In effect, this applied the language of Mill' s Legitimacy Test, or Harm Criterion. But this language proved too strong for respectable governments and politicians on the eve of the third millennium!

There has been a continuing campaign for wider measures 123 to ensure access to information, and the campaigners have argued for the consistent and legally binding application of this' test of harm'. Mill had argued that the only ground for limiting liberty was' harm' – now the campaigners argued that where no such harm was evident, information should automatically flow into the public domain.

In 1998, the New Labour Government of Tony Blair drew 124 up a plan, involving a freedom of information commissioner, with the power to require an authority to consider revealing information' in the public interest' – but not the power to enforce that release of information.

125 Jack Straw, the minister responsible, saw a great widening of access to information, and so of free debate:

> **QUOTATION**
>
> ...the bill requires an authority to consider disclosing information, taking into account all the circumstances of the case, including the public interest.

126 Critics replied acerbically that: ' *Ministers would decide* **if it is in the public interest** *to reveal information.* ' This is the core issue. *Who* decides on' the public interest' ? The Government argued that it must be responsible for regulating the flow of information, and hence of discussion: ' *to leave these decisions to the Information Commissioner would be "profoundly unclemocratic".* '

127 The argument is precisely the one Mill anticipated in his 1859 discussion. The government is democratically elected, and so it has the right to decide on the limits of public freedom of discussion. Indeed, the government is you acting here on behalf of the public. We have here an example of Mill's history of freedom. An inherited understanding of liberty is now out of context. In the new phase, the old concept backfires.

128 Already in 1859, Mill was arguing that democracy could become the basis for a resurgence of censorship of public discussion. The old concepts of liberty had arisen in protest at traditional tyranny by kings or aristocrats. Why

shouldn't a publicly elected regime restrict discussion in line with its popular mandate?Why shouldn't ministers decide what is in the public interest to reveal, subject to appropriate checks and scrutiny?For example, would it really be in the public interest to know the details of reports on possible petrol shortages before they became truly relevant?Wouldn't that simply cause panic and trigger a crisis?Would it be in the public interest to reveal sensitive debates about the handling of peace negotiations, say in Northern Ireland?

Yet all such information has, in effect, the potential for discussion. In restricting the information, a twenty-first-century government is limiting public debate just as surely as any earlier regime, though with less brutality. Mill does not give a simple yes/no answer to any specific question. You can't discover in *On Liberty* the recipe for deciding whether specific data about a remote risk to public health should be rdeased while the experts remain divided. However, Mill encourages a state of mind which is sceptical towards official justifications of censorship, including censorship by data management.

Mill's classic analysis of liberty of the press looks back to the seventeenth century, and points forward into the twenty-first century.

# Hearing the Arguments

131  Now we examine Mill's arguments on 'liberty of thought and discussion' throughout the main body of his second chapter. Throughout the analysis. we are going to see how Mill cuts away, one after another, the reasons which seem to justify restricting liberty of thought and discussion. The whole chapter is a process of elimination. We are left with his own principle of liberty, the Harm Criterion.

132  This method produces a distinctive intellectual excitement. Mill's own reasoning enacts his belief in the need for the collision of ideas. In his other works, Mill was also a leading theorist of logic, and the second chapter of *On Liberty* is a great example of Mill's own art of thinking, which one might also call 'the art of seeing ideas whole'.

> **MILL'S ART OF THINKING**
>
> * *The method of reasonable extremism.* Mill demands that
>   we take the whole of an argument through to its conclusion
>   and do not stop short where it seems' sensible' to us.
>
> * *The dialectical approach to ideas.* Mill requires us to see
>   each idea from as many points of view as possible, inclu-
>   ding as many hostile points of view as possible. Thinking is
>   the art of taking into account every possible objection.

If we do not follow an argument as far as it can go, and if 133
we do not entertain every serious objection, then we cannot be said to have understood that argument. This is a
demanding standard of reasoning, and Mill's own practice
is its greatest defence.

Throughout his argument, Mill will be demanding that we 134
listen to the views of those who seem to us offensive, destructive, wrong, mad, cranky and irrelevant. The argument has a human core. To illustrate we will be bringing in
a few modern character types.

### *Purist*

A *purist* will never compromise. He or she has the key to 135
life, the answer to every problem. Other people usually assume that ' Purist' is a kind of irrelevance. Do we really
need to listen? Can' t we just, in the most polite way, delete
this tiresome and obsessive viewpoint from public debate?

### Extremist

136 An *extremist* is drawn to take up exactly the position that is most offensive to everyone else. Whatever the mainstream view, 'Extremist' will be found proclaiming the reverse. He or she will never use a mild word where an abusive one is available. The mark of an extremist is that he or she assumes an argument is good when everyone is offended or outraged.

### Paranoiac

137 A *paranoiac* believes there is a plot at work. Everyone else is deceived but he or she knows the hidden secret. 'Paranoiac' tends to focus on a single issue or explanation. To the mainstream eye, Paranoiac is the least rational of all these outsiders.

138 Mill's argument is effectively written as a dialogue, though he does not give the other side a name. We might call this adversary 'Normal', the voice of a commonsense which cannot imagine the need for any other views or voices. Normal generally suggests that we do not need to hear from such types as Purist, Extremist and Paranoiac – that their voices mess up proper discussion and distort public debate. They poison the atmosphere, they distract attention from the real issues and they are anyway impossible to argue with. Of course, we may not believe in locking them up – though sometimes we might – but we know there are

many other ways to keep such voices silent, at least as far
as public discussion is concerned.

In his argument, Mill imagines a number of arguments that 139
a Normal type might use against free discussion:

* *The Unanimity Argument*: ' But everyone else agrees! '

* *The Absurdity Argument*: ' I won' t listen to this non-
  sense! '

* *The Offended Argument*: ' But that' s outrageous! '

* *The Threatened Argument*: ' That idea threatens the
  foundations of decent society! '

* *The Confident Argument*: ' But we already know the
  truth! '

Against these propositions, Mill argues not only that we 140
should tolerate dissenting characters and weird ideas in
our public life – but also that we absolutely need them.

# THE UNANIMITY ARGUMENT:
# ' BUT EVERYONE ELSE AGREES! '

To Normal, it seems obvious that where everyone agrees, 141
there is no need to tolerate futile objections. Free discussion has its limits, and one of them is where society has
made up its mind. Mill replies on behalf of all extremists,
purists, paranoiacs and other exceptions:

## Anatomy of the Key Quote

o '*minus one*' : For Mill, the reasonable extremist, the exception has equal weight with the rule.

o '*of one opinion*' : That would-be unanimity is the ideal
form of public opinion. This state is the goal of every
'public'.

142 Take the case of' the Last Marxist', a contemporary form
of purist. Let' s say nobody else believes in Marxist principles any more. We all think the Cold War was won 20 years
ago. Do we really have to listen to this voice, endlessly explaining why the Class War is still going on, why imperial-
ism is the cause of world poverty?Can' t society simply re-
fuse to invite the Last Marxist along to the party?He can
simply be left off all the agendas, kept away from every
episode of *Question Time* turned away from all publishers'
lists and so on. This in Mill' s terms is absolutely wrong. We
are no more entitled to shut the Last Marxist up than he or
she is to silence the rest of the world.

143 Here we can see Mill drawing simultaneously on the Liberal Legitimacy Test and the Appeal to Utility. If the exception does no harm, the rest of mankind is not entitled to

suppress his voice: that is the logical consequence of flow-
ing through the Harm Criterion. The appeal to utility adds
a positive angle:

---

**KEY QUOTE**

But the peculiar evil of silencing an opinion is, that it is robbing the human race, posterity as well as the existing generation – those who dissent from the opinion still more than those
who hold it.

---

○ '*. . . robbing the human race*' : This is probably the single
most important phrase in Mill's defence of freedom of
thought and discussion. If we decide to keep a voice quiet, then we are damaging the interests of the whole of
humanity.

○ '*posterity as well as the existing generation*' : Mill defined utility as 'the permanent interests' of humanity as a
'progressive' species. Here he applies that standard
positively: ideas are forever, censorship violates the
rights of the future to decide for itself!

Take an example. For many of us, one of the most boring 144
forms of 'extremist' is 'the only man', the Last True Male.
Would pushing the off switch on this voice really be robbing humanity? Do we need to give airtime to his brilliant
discoveries that masculinity has been betrayed, or that he
alone has the right to whatever he wants? According to
Mill, humanity does need this voice, as it needs every other
voice: '*If the opinion is right*' then we have lost out on an

opportunity to discover the truth. But more important, if the opinion is wrong:

---

**KEY QUOTE**

...they lose, what is almost as great a benefit, the clearer perception and livelier impression of truth produced by its collision with error.

---

**Anatomy of the Key Quote**

○ ' *its collision*' : This is a clear statement of dialectic. Ideas need their opposites to flourish.

○ ' *benefit*' : The terms ' benefit' and ' cost' have become central to the analysis and assessment of welfare.

○ ' *impression*' : This term has a long history in English philosophy and poetry, including Wordsworth, Mill's much-loved romantic poet. An impression is the subjective impact of the moment of perception.

# THE ABSURDITY ARGUMENT: ' I WON' T LISTEN TO THIS NONSENSE! '

145 Normal has plenty of other arguments against free discussion. Why should someone sensible have to put up with the intrusion of views that are patently ridiculous? This is the Absurdity Argument, a common alternative to the Unanimity argument. Mill replies with his own brand of extremist

reasoning!

> **QUOTATION**
>
> We can never be sure that the opinion we are endeavouring to stifle is a false opinion.

This is a strong view, which goes a lot further than most 146 people would follow. Normal, and his or her philosophical representatives, would ask: Can we really never be sure that an opinion is false?

Take Paranoiac at his or her most extravagant. There are 147 plenty of contemporary examples. For instance, Paranoiac believes that the United Nations is trying to take over A-merica, or that baby food is you being sold which is you known to be unsafe. The problem is that sometimes Para-noiac does seem to hit the target and the mainstream then looks complacent or worse. Mill isn't saying that Paranoiac is likely to be right. He is allowing a space.

Answering the Absurdity Argument, Mill comes up with a 148 classic statement:

> **KEY QUOTE**
>
> All silencing of discussion is an assumption of infallibility.

### Anatomy of the Key Quote

○ ' *infallibility*' : This key word has a long history in religious

and political conflict going back to the Protestant refor-
mation and the Catholic view of papal authority. The
Pope took upon himself the status of being infallible, with
regard to religious doctrine. Protestantism was born partly in reaction to this notion of papal infallibility. But Mill insists it is common for people to assume they are infallible
without realizing it. ' *Every time you keep someone else
out of the discussion, you are effectively assuming that
you are infallible.* '

○ ' *assumption*' : One of the functions of modern logic is to
reveal and discredit the hidden assumptions of ordinary
arguments. Mill-the-logician is the enemy of the latent
assumption.

149 In effect, Mill is applying his Liberal Legitimacy Test to the
would-be censors. Even if an idea is absurd, what harm is
it doing? He is also resorting, perhaps more forcefully, to
the Utility Appeal:

> **QUOTATION**
>
> . . . the opinion which it is attempted to suppress by authority
> may possibly be true. Those who desire to suppress it, of
> course deny its truth; but they are not infallible.

150 This argument is subtler than it looks. At first glance. one
thinks: this is ' liberal relativism' , that is, the view that there
is no absolute truth, only different points of view. We have
to accept other points of view, because there *are only*

*viewpoints*. There is no such thing as the truth; therefore everyone gets to put a point of view. In fact, Mill is not that kind of liberal at all. His objection to would-be infallibility is founded on his love of truth, not on mere acceptance of different viewpoints. He takes truth extremely seriously. It is because we are trying genuinely to get closer to the truth about an issue, that we cannot afford to rule out of court any arguments in advance.

The truth may be a limit towards which we reach but which 151 we never attain – but the journey is still serious. It is a sign of our good faith in any discussion, our commitment to finding the truth out, that we let all the voices join in, even the ones which seem to us most far-fetched, most offensive, most destructive.

Here Mill is doing far more than object to censorship. He is 152 also making a positive case. We could say that he is establishing the standards for genuine discussion, and so for an authentic public culture, but Mill allows the other side to object, what about ideas that are 'dangerous' as well as absurd? After all, the two may go together, from a normal perspective. Are there not, he asks on behalf of his critics, some views that are '*dangerous to the welfare of mankind, either in this life or another*'? In that case, the Utility appeal would work the other way round, as a basis for censorship.

### The medical panic: a fictional scenario

Take, in our time, a group of Paranoiac Extremists, who 153

combine the wild obsession of the one with the deliberate offensiveness of the other. They go around arguing that modern medicine is a vast conspiracy. It is not safe to give any medical treatment, and particularly not to children. They begin to make headway. Worried parents are keeping their children away from clinics and doctors on an increasing scale. There are signs that this is causing the beginning of a serious epidemic and deterioration in infant mortality figures. Is there not a strong case for trying to silence these views, for the good of the children?

154 Every expert agrees that this panic is you based on lies, distortions and misconceptions. Does the government not have a duty to try to suppress this panic-inducing campaign?Perhaps there should be a new charge of falsely inducing public panic?Or maybe there should be simply a concerted campaign of vilification against this group? Perhaps the media should refrain from giving them space?Mill would resist that we have to faca out the argument, even with these Paranoiac Extremists. Of course, if they start attacking clinics, or sending letter bombs to doctors, then they have violated the liberty of others and they fall foul of the Harm Criterion. But if they are genuinely arguing their 'mad' case, we have to meet them on that ground. The reason is that somewhere in their chaotic rant, there may be something true, something neglected. Alternatively, we may discover the true basis for our faith in medical treatment more clearly by refuting them.

## The BSE scandal: a historical scenario

In reply, you might say, that is you a fantasy case: it illus-   155
trates the ideas in theory, but in practice we are too grown
up to censor silly arguments on the grounds that they are
dangerous. However, there are many different versions of
' silencing' and some of them do seem to play a part in the
regulation of our public debates.

Take a current case: the BSE controversy. This is a classic   156
illustration of Mill' s main points: first, that society is always
keen to silence awkward views; second, that there are
many ways of silencing unwanted viewpoints; and third,
that one can never be sure that what seems to be a mar-
ginal and extreme view will not turn out to have weight, e-
ven in an apparently scientific issue. When the first voices
were raised in the UK about the spread of infection to hu-
mans, they were generally treated with contempt. There
were cases where experts lost grants, or were threatened
with the loss of their jobs, or actually lost their iobs. The
media coverage of these ' prophets of doom' was mocking
or worse. All of these are examples of modern censorship
- our ways to silence then unwanted argument. This case
also illustrates vividly Mill' s positive point, for here it did indeed turn out that some at least of the far-fetched claims
needed to be taken seriously. Such examples illustrate
Mill' s argument that utility and liberty are inseparable. Free
discussion is in the interests of mankind.

# THE OFFENDED ARGUMENT:
# 'BUT THAT'S OUTRAGEOUS!'

157 There are plenty of other 'Normal' arguments for censoring free discussion. The most heated of all is the 'Offended Argument'. This is where someone, speaking for the mainstream, declares that an individual or a minority is offending their deepest sensibilities.

158 Mill is not going to argue merely for tolerating offensive views, he insists that we should actually welcome and even encourage them. In the end, the argument focuses on religious and moral blasphemy. To explain his approach, he starts with a 'cool' example:

> **KEY QUOTE**
>
> If even the Newtonian philosophy were not permitted to be questioned, mankind could not feel as complete assurance of its truth as they now do.

## Anatomy of the Key Quote

○ '*the Newtonian philosophy*' : Newton's Laws of Motion had been scientific gospel since the seventeenth century and include the Law of Gravit. In this argument, though, the 'Newtonian philosophy' stands for any Great Truth, which has worked its way into the whole outlook of a society.

o ' *even*' : This is not really an argument about gravity. The word ' even' turns this example into a kind of' limit case' What Mill means is that society considers it unacceptable to question other kinds of Great Truth which, by implication, are less secure than the Newtonian philosophy.

The more important a Great Truth seems, the more essential it is to allow others to challenge it. The reason is that if nobody ever denies ' even' the law of gravity, it will cease to have any real meaning. We will stop thinking about it. Mill then gives the example of the Catholic Church that arranges for a devil' s advocate to argue against the canonlzatlon of any new proposed saint. Every Great Truth should have an equivalent role. 159

Mill now introduces into the argument the important term, ' extreme' , and gives a defence of the need to apply freedom to what arc seen as the most extreme views at any given time. Here he is taking on, face to face, the' Offended Argument' for censorship: 160

**KEY QUOTE**

Strange it is that men should admit the validity of the arguments for free discussion, but object to their being ' pushed to an extreme' , not seeing that unless the reasons are good for an extreme case, they are not good for any case.

## Anatomy of the Key Quote

- ' *admit the validity*' : People are reluctant to accept the basis for uncensored expression. There is a sense of working against the grain throughout this section of *On Liberty*.

- ' *an extreme*' : People want to keep a ' sensible' limit on free discussion, even though they have no valid argument for doing so. ' Extreme' , here, indicates that Mill is moving on to consider those ideas and viewpoints that strike the mainstream as too outrageous, as offensive in their very existence.

161 So Mill insists that if a society is you serious about free discussion, it will actively encourage the most unacceptable views to be expressed openly and clearly. He confronts our Normal face to face. For Normal there are certain values that are beyond challenge. To doubt them is to commit a sin: ' *none but bad men would desire to weaken these salutary beliefs*' .

162 In our time, such Great Truths might include ' family values' or ' work is good for you' . Consider the abusive representation of those who challenge family values – an abuse which Mill would count as a form of censorship. In this context, Mill uses blasphemy and heresy as positive terms: they represent challenges to established assumptions, without which there is you no scope for change. He then turns to religious examples of offensive views:

---

**QUOTATION**

Let the opinions impugned be the belief in a God and in a future state, or any of the commonly received doctrines of morality.

---

God and morality go together. Is it simply morally unac-　163
ceptable to question these sacred beliefs?Sacred beliefs
are really the fertile ground for Extremist. You cannot think
of a cherished befief that will not attract critical invective.
Certainly this is likely to get pretty offensive to the believ-
ers, whether in God or in the family or in heterosexual decency. But after all, who counts as an extremist may
change depending on the perspective. The first great philosopher, Socrates, was put to death for subverting the established moral beliefs of Achens. ' *Mankind can hardly be
too often reminded that there was once a man called Socrates*' .

More contentiously, there is the case or Jesus himself:　164

---

**QUOTATION**

The man who left on the memory of those who witnessed his
life and conversation, such an impression of his moral gran-
deur that eighteen subsequent centuries have done homage
to him as the Almighty in person, was ignominiously put to
death, as what?As a blasphemer.

---

Here Mill is deepening his defence of blasphemy as pos-　165
sessing positive utility. If we look beyond the present mo-

ment, if we see the vista of history, then we realize we cannot be sure how a person or his views will appear. There seems to be reason to think that the most creative figures in history will strike their own time as blasphemous. Precisely those views that lead to real change and advancement, will be most offensive to their own day. How could it be otherwise?

166 Here again the basis for the defence of liberty is you a dialectical view of history. We need counter-ideas to oppose the present orthodoxy, otherwise humanity will be frozen. We cannot take it upon ourselves to decide which extremist in our day will turn out to be the herald of human progress, and which will be a mere nuisance. In fact, it is probably true that most times Extremist is just a pain. The trouble is, occasionally he or she is the new age calling.

167 The Offended Argument for censorship is one of the most dangerous. First, Mill insists, cutting out Extremists violates the Liberal Legitimacy Test. They are doing no 'harm to others', except for upsetting the mainstream. Second, and more importantly, Mill applies his Appeal to Utility. Extremism may turn out to be in the long-term interests of the growth of the human race. Nobody can be sure at the time whether this particular outrageous view will turn out to have such historical utility.

# THE THREATENED ARGUMENT: 'THAT IDEA THREATENS THE FOUNDATIONS OF DECENT SOCIETY!'

Are any values necessary for the survival of society?Here 168
the Victorian critic James Stephen was particularly outraged: obviously, he proclaimed, society must protect its
basic values from attack!For Mill, this question follows from
the previous discussion of heretics. For example, Mill re-
calls, the Roman Emperor Marcus Aurelius suppressed
Christianity because he believed it would undermine decent Roman society:

---

**KEY QUOTE**

...he saw, or thought he saw that it [society] was held together, and prevented from being worse, by belief and rev-
erence of the received divinities.

---

### Anatomy of the Key Quote

- ' *held together...by belief* ' : This is a common assumption: that certain beliefs glue society together. Where
  these beliefs are concerned, social unity takes precedence over liberty.

- ' *the received divinities* ' : In Roman times, the pagan
  gods presided over the central institutions of society. Mill

is being satirical. In later times, there are different founding dogmas: the nation, the monarchy.

169 Marcus Aurelius was a decent man and a genuine philosopher. However, he is an enemy of liberty because he de-
nied freedom to an ideology that' openly aimed at dissol-
ving ties'. This is the Threatened Argument for censorship. Certain ideas are too subversive. Society is too fragile
to permit absolutely free discussion.

170 Mill's attack on this Threatened Argument follows on from
his defence of heretics against mainstream outrage. In the
main, the subversives have been people of good faith.
They know that as dissidents they must preserve a higher
standard of decency in order not to discredit their ideas in
the eyes of the mainstream:

> **QUOTATION**
>
> . . . it is historically true that a large portion of infidels in all a-
> ges have been persons of distinguished integrity and honour.

171 The Threatened Argument works by instilling fear, both in
the majority and in the dissidents. We are standing on the
brink of social collapse; let's all cling together and hang
on to the beliefs that keep us safe. In that oppressive atmosphere, minorities fall silent and keep their views to
themselves:

╔══════════════════════════════════════╗

**KEY QUOTE**

Those in whose eyes this reticence on the part of heretics is no evil should consider. . . that in consequence of it there is never any fair and thorough discussion of heretical opinions.

╚══════════════════════════════════════╝

## Anatomy of the Key Quote

○ ' *reticence*' : Merely making people hesitate to speak is enough to suppress free discussion. All censorship is total censorship.

○ ' *fair and thorough*' : Only in a free discussion can the heresy be refuted. If the outsiders aren' t refuted, they will never learn. If we don' t try to refute them, we will never learn the limits of the mainstream.

Two key points emerge from Mill' s discussion of social co- 172 herence and freedom.

1 There is no such thing as a partly free discussion.

2 There is never a case for the utility of suppressing a viewpoint. The Threatened Argument for censorship suggests that society as a whole may be better off if certain views are kept silent. Mill, however, replies that the effect is a loss of well-being on both sides – censors and censored.

# THE CONFIDENT ARGUMENT: 'BUT WE ALREADY KNOW THE TRUTH!'

173 Surely if what' we' say is true, there is no need for us to listen to the other side?Mill goes to work by successive arguments to undermine this apparently plausible and commonsensical position. He comes up with a series of vivid formulations to make us look again at the very words' true' and' truth' :

> **QUOTATION**
>
> Popular opinions. . . are often true, but seldom or never the whole truth. Heretical opinions. . . are generally some of these suppressed and neglected truths.

174 Mill' s argument is about truth and history.

* Heresy is often the other side of truth, the side unseen by a particular period.

* The truth is dialectical: it consists of the endless play of oppositions. To limit that play is to block the path to illumination.

175 Heresy is, Mill insists, often the more urgent side of the truth for any given period. The familiar aspect of truth is liable to be less helpful than the one we have been avoiding: ' *The new fragment of truth is more wanted, more adapted to the needs of the time than that which it displaces*' .

Mill seeks to confront us with the sheer scale of the truth. 176
as a field far larger than conventional thinking has assumed. His argument is comparable with nineteenth-century discoveries about time. Previously, time had been thought of on a more or less human scale: the earth and the universe belonged to a humanly comprehensible story. However, Victorian geology and biology replaced this narrow view of time with a sense of ' deep time ' – notably in Darwin' s *Origin of Species.* Mill is arguing for a similar revision in the understanding of truth, a sense of how deep and broad the truth must be, how far it extends in all directions beyond our ordinary beliefs and ideas.

Mill devotes a specific discussion to Christian ethics. They 177
are valid, but incomplete. Originally, it was Christianity that expressed a necessary heresy, the side of ethical truth hidden from classical ethics, which insisted on service to society and overlooked personal salvation: ' *Christian ethics. . . they contain, and were meant to contain, only a part ofthe truth.* '

We tend to think of ethics as a matter of opinion, but Mill 178
thinks of different ethical systems as contributions to a dialectical argument about truth. In this regard, his thinking resembles that of another great Victorian liberal, Matthew Arnold, who proposed a famous division between Hebraic and Hellenic systems.

Mill ends this ethical argument by insisting that his goal is 179
' *the mental well-being of mankind*' . Well-being is the main theme in his next chapter.

# Free to be Human: Mill's Proverbs of Well-being

180 Chapter Ⅲ of *On Liberty* is called' Of Individuality'. In this section of the guide, we shall see how, for Mill, individuality is the bedrock of the argument about freedom. Every argument stops somewhere, – where, as the contemporary philosopher Hilary Putnam says, the spade eventually touches the bedrock. Even the most sophisticated chain of reasoning has an ending, a point beyond which the reasons will not take you. In Mill's case, that resting point is' individuality'. If you ask, what is the point of freedom?, the answer at the end of the chain of reasons is: freedom enables us to be individuals, to be ourselves.

181 We can see that Mill has reached a different phase of his argument, because he adopts a new style. In his earlier chapters, he writes in a reasoning voice which:

  * makes connections between ideas;

* answers objections to ideas.

Now another voice enters, or becomes more audible. This　182
is a **proverbial voice**. The third chapter is full of sayings or
near-sayings. In some ways, the writing is more like a rea-
sonable-seeming version of Oscar Wilde than a ' normal
philosopher' . Why does Mill speak in this proverbial voice?
He has reached some end-points in his reasoning. These
are not arbitrary claims, they are still linked to reasons, but
they are also where the reasons come to rest. These sayings are reason' s points of homecoming. Therefore, Mill
naturally expresses such ideas in a more final-sounding
style. At the same time, the sayings are also provocative.
Though understated, the proverbs are in their way as outrageous, for conventional opinion, as anything in Wilde or
Nietzsche.

# INDIVIDUALITY AND WELL-BEING

Consider first the full chapter heading: ' *Of Individiduality,*　183
*as One of the Elements of Well-Being*' . Mill is not, in the
end, going to defend individuality on moral or political
grounds. The whole argument culminates in a theory of human well-being.

---

**The grounds of freedom**

Liberty permits individuality. Without individuality, there is no
well-being.

---

184 There is a clear line of reasoning. Without liberty, we cannot be ourselves, or even find out where to look for our true selves. Well-being consists of being yourself, as fully as possible. Who would argue against well-being? According to Mill, most conventional values violate human well-being because they attempt to suppress the expression of individuality. Most people hold moralistic views of the human condition, which demand that people conform to some externally fixed standard or criterion of the good life, the best way of living. *On Liberty* now conducts an intellectual war against that moralistic paradigm.

185 Mill's view of freedom is still radical because it sweeps aside moralistic thinking, on behalf of the bedrock notion of human well-being. No one is entitled to tell you what makes for your own individual well-being. By ' **individuality** ', therefore, Mill means the reverse of conformity. We have seen in the previous chapter, how his defence of free discussion is based upon the argument for diversity. We need as many different ideas and arguments as possible for a healthy society. Only through conflict and contrast does intellectual progress occur. The truth itself leaves space for different and conflicting ideas. Now he extends the same dialectical outlook to his treatment of individual lives.

---

**The logic of liberty**

If individuality produces well-being, then conformity is bad for you.

---

Throughout, we have raised the question of Mill' s utilitarian 186
theory and how it relates to his argument about liberty. In
his treatment of individuality, Mill is both an advocate of liberty and a utilitarian. Well-being is a more subtle and humane version of the utilitarian concept of happiness. Freedom is good because it enhances well-being and therefore
is useful, in this philosophical sense of spreading genuine
happiness, relieving genuine frustration.

In what follows, we pick out the key sayings that are scat- 187
tered through this great chapter on individual well-being,
as if they made up a' dictionary of well-being' .

## MILL' S PROVERBS OF WELL-BEING

> **QUOTATION**
>
> THE FIRST PROVERB OF WELL – BEING
> Men should be free to act upon their opinions

### Mill' s Dictionary of Well-Being

○ ' *Being free*' means that you can act upon your opinions.
  It is not enough to be able to hold or even express an o-
  pinion, if you are prevented from acting on it. Therefore,
  freedom of opinion includes being able to act.

○ ' *Freedom to*' is as important as' freedom from' . In fact,
  you could say that' freedom to' is the point. the pay-off of

' freedom from' . Being free from interference is the negative half of being free to act. This proverb of well-being is
about' freedom to' – the preceding arguments about
public discussion focused on ' freedom from' .

○ ' *Their opinions*' : A person cannot truly be said to hold
their own opinions if they cannot express them in practice. This is the full meaning of opinion.

## Implications

### *Authentication*

188 An opinion is not authentic if the holder is not able to act
on it. Mill is a rational thinker and one tends to associate
authenticity with more romantic spirits, say, Nietzsche or
D. H. Lawrence. However, as we have seen, Mill is very
much an advocate of authenticity. You could see this as
part of the Victorian intellectuals' opposition to what they
saw as the hypocrisy of their age. If people are forbidden
to act on their opinion, then they are effectively turned into
hypocrites. After a time, such a society will produce people
who do not know whether they are sincere or not, whether
they really believe an opinion or are just playing.

### *The science of opinion*

189 This proverb also has a scientific aspect. If you cannot act
on your opinions, it is like a science that is restricted to
mere hypotheses – you will never test them. In effect, opinions are moral hypotheses or psychological hypotheses or
political hypotheses. Acts are the experiments that test

these hypotheses. If I cannot act on my opinion, I am being deprived, too, of the opportunity to refute it.

## Qualifications

Mill qualifies this proverb in two ways:                              190

1 *Positively*. The obstacles to this freedom of action are twofold: physical or moral. We need to be free from both these hindrances if we are truly to lay down the foundations for our own lives. Morality is no diffierent from phyrsical restraint. This negative morality is simply a way of restricting the lives of others. Morality becomes a prison-house.

2 *Negatively*. Mill adds that people are free to act on their opinion ' at their own risk' . This links him with a strong current in contemporary social and ethical thought, where' risk' has become a central topic. For Mill, risk is integral to freedom. A free person can take chances with his or her own life. If you are not allowed to take risks, then you are not an autonomous individual: that is one of the dividing lines between children and adults.

A free society cannot remove risk from the lives of its citi-  191
zens. Without risks, there can be no individuality. Society cannot make people lead safe lives.

┌─────────────────────────────────────────┐
│ **QUOTATION**
│
│ THE SECOND PROVERB OF WELL-BEING
│
│ while mankind are imperfect. . . there should be different ex-
│ periments of living
└─────────────────────────────────────────┘

## Mill's Dictionary of Well-Being

○ '*Imperfect*' : There is a characteristic irony: will mankind ever be anything else? But the point is also a serious one: humanity evolves and we may approach closer to perfection than we are at present. Either way, mankind will need variety: that is the source of change.

○ '*Experiments*' : It is as if our lives are scientific projects. Each genuinely free individual makes his or her own hypothesis about the good life. Such lives are like scientific experiments: they test out a theory in practice. Just as science eliminates errors and makes new discoveries through such testing, so our practical knowledge also advances. 'Experimental' also implies something new, something original: there is a link with the previous idea of 'risk'.

## Implications

192 In a free society, there is you a dialectic of life choices, a contest between contrasting life visions. Each person makes his or her own life choice and then there is effectively a competition between these alternatives. This con-

test serves a purpose in the historical development of humanity. Over time, it emerges that this choice is productive, that one is flawed. Mill talks about these experiments as being 'useful' : 'he is applying utility' to the question of individual choice. Humanity as a whole will benefit if individuals are free to experiment with their lives. Though each person may gain or lose, mankind as a whole will be better off. Cumulatively, there will be more well-being in the world, if people are allowed to test out alternative lifestyles.

History is the only legitimate judge of the value of a life 193 choice. Has that way of living proved beneficial to humanity?

> **QUOTATION**
>
> THE THIRD PROVERB OF WELL-BEING
>
> it is the privilege and proper condition of a human being . . . to use and interpret experience in his own way

## Mill's Dictionary of Well-Being

○ ' *The privilege and proper condition*' : Mill does not invoke the idea of 'rights' in his argument for freedom. He does not argue that we have a human right to be free, but he does see humanity as having a 'proper condition' , which is defined by liberty. The word condition is originally medical: to be in good condition means to be healthy. This right condition is a part of our human well-being. Though we don't have rights, in Mill's argument, our human nature can only express itself in certain environments. The word 'privilege' feels ironic in this context. Nobody grants us the privilege of our humanity: it is simply ours by nature.

○ ' *Interpret*' : Interpretation is a central theme of modern thought. For example, it is the theme of Freud's theories, which begin with his *Interpretation of Dreams*. We make life our own by giving it our meaning. Interpretation turns what happens to me into *my* experience. Through interpretation, we live life from the inside. Meaning gives the 'mine-ness' to my life. Mill couples 'interpret' with 'use' : there is nothing fanciful or abstract about interpretation. If we cannot give meaning to our lives, we are unable to make use of them.

## Implications

194 If human beings interpret their own lives, they are being 'reflexive'. Mill is arguing that our liberty includes the scope to be fully self-reflexive. This links him with later thinkers. including some of the most influential in our time. notably the sociologist Anthony Giddens and the theorist of 'risk society', Ulrich Beck.

195 No wonder Mill's reputation is on the rise. These are the criteria of postmodern liberty. In this theory of well-being, Mill becomes the precursor of postmodern doctrines of liberty. Whereas his theory of free speech was the most influ-

ential and controversial aspect of *On Liberty* in modern times, his theory of individuality is likely to be his most influential idea for postmodern times. Mill' s *On Liberty* sees **self-reflexiveness** as part of well-being. It is thus justified both by the Liberal Legitimacy Test – it harms nobody – and by utility – it creates new possibilities of human experience.

> **Mill and postmodern liberty**
>
> We must be free to interpret our own lives. Liberty is self-relexive.

> **QUOTATION**
>
> THE FOURTH PROVERB OF WELL-BEING
>
> the . . . customs of other people are evidence of what their experience has taught them

## Mill' s Dictionary of Well-Being

○ ' *Customs*' : Mill defines' custom' as a second-hand interpretation of experience. To the extent that I follow custom. I am living a borrowed life, or living life on borrowed meanings. Custom is the alternative to interpreting experience for myself. More positively, the customs of others could be a useful ingredient in my search for my own interpretation, if regarded from outside. So, that is what they made of their experience; how well does that fit with my understanding of my own life?

## Qualifications

196 Mill recognizes that these customs may embody a 'correct' understanding of someone else's experience. In other words, he is not the kind of thinker who sees all customs and traditions as wrong. Mill is not a crude modernizer. He does not think that custom is wrong because it is old-fashioned, or that the new will automatically be better. His argument is that custom may have been right for someone else, from their perspective on their own experience, but it still has to be tested afresh in each new life. The old understanding may be correct but 'unsuitable' for me.

## Implications

197 Mill does not object to custom in itself. His objection is to compulsory custom, or tradition with a moral edge. If a society imposes customs, then it is also requiring people to interpret their lives in certain ways. Why should each generation live according to the self-understanding of their ancestors? In other words, Mill's case is that rigid customs deprive humanity of the new meanings that would arise if people were left to think for themselves. A custom-based society contributes fewer meanings to the history of mankind than an open society.

198 For instance, in the past, certain groups experienced their sexuality in the form of temptation. Others may experience

sexuality as self-expression. One community may experience as solidarity what I experience as monotony. Your
distraction may be my opportunity. Your irrelevance may
be my new world. In Mill's terms, neither side can turn
round to the other and insist that it possesses the only true
interpretation. There is you no right answer. The question,
within the limits of harm to others, is which interpretation is
' suitable' to me.

---

**QUOTATION**

THE FIFTH PROVERB OF WELL-BEING

He who does anything because it is the custom makesno
choice.

---

## Mill ' s Dictionary of Well-Being

○ ' *Choice*' : Choice has become one of the main concepts
in contemporary political and moral debate. Here is another example of Mill' s increasing relevance to the future. He offers sharp definitions of the terms we are
struggling to focus on ourselves. For Mill, choice is a
function of individuality. A true choice expresses my nature, and not my way of belonging with others.

○ ' *No choice*' : Mill produces a theory of false or inauthent-
ic choice. A custom-based society reduces, or eliminates, true choice. If people select on the basis of traditions, then they are not becoming individuals.

**Implications**

* *All choice is personal.*

* *More choice means greater individuality.*

199 These views are actually quite extreme by ordinary standards. How often do people really ignore the usual judgements or requirements? How commonly do we really
choose without any reference to the norm? According to
Mill, true choice is difficult.

200 Modern politicians and economists often talk about exten-
ding choice or about glvmg people wider choices. For
Mill, many of these choices would be deceptive. He would
not be happy to accept conventional views of' consumer
choice' for example. because most of thc time consumers
choose within a tightly defined set of norms – fashion,
say, or status or the values imposed by advertising. By
Mill's standards, contemporary lifestyle would be no better
than traditional customs. In fact, lifestyle would simply be a
kind of instantaneous and short-lived custom.

201 According to Mill, we cannot say a society is free if people
choose what is customary. Equally, a society is unfree if
people choose only what is recommended by the adverts,
or what impresses the neighbours. One example would be
deciding to have children. If people have children because
that is what they are meant to do, then they are making, in
Mill's terms, ' no choice' .

> ### QUOTATION
>
> THE SIXTH PROVERB OF WELL-BEING
>
> desires and impulses are as much a part of a perfect human being, as beliefs and restraints

## Mill' s Dictionary of Well-Being

○ ' *Desires and impulses*' : Here again, Mill seems to anticipate Freud and modern psychology. Repressing desire makes us less human, not more civilized. Having no spontaneous impulses makes us wooden, not self-possessed.

○ ' *A perfect human being*' : This is an ideal, though not a recipe. Mill does propose and defend certain ways of being human against other ways. He does not believe that we will ever achieve perfection, but he has an ideal standard by which he judges. By perfection, MIll means the fullest possible expression of human nature—the more human, the better, within the rule of no harm to others.

### Implications

There is a dialectic of well-being. Mill is not arguing that all 202 desire is good, that we must act on impulse all the time. On the contrary, he is saying that we need both desire and belief, both impulse and restraint. In this argument, belief refers to considered views and judgements, formed in discussion with others. Desire is the immediate expression of a personal will, an instinctive force or drive. True self-control is achieved through the relationship between desire and belief, impulse and restraint. A person who eliminates desire is not showing self-control at all: what does he or she have to control in the first place?

203 Mill adds that strong impulses are not dangerous in themselves. They only become a problem if they are not' properly balanced'. Nobody without strong desires will ever develop true self-control. Why would they need to? Both self-control and desire are part of our experience of humanity.

204 Here we can see that Mill both is and is not a relativist. He is a relativist in the sense that he will not impose on others a model for how to be a good human, but he is not a relativist, in that he defends a certain approach to the good life, an approach based on this idea of' a perfect human being' as the fullest possible expression of every side of our nature, within the limits of harm to others. The more we approach perfection, the greater will be the utility of our lives in the vista of human history.

---

**QUOTATION**

THE SEVENTH PROVERB OF WELL-BEING

There is no natural connection between strong impulses and a weak conscience.

---

## Mill's Dictionary of Well-Being

○ '*Conscience*': Throughout *On Liberty*, Mill argues a-
gainst moralistic attitudes to other people. Most people'
s morality is a device for judging others, for rationalizing
their dislike of what is different or challenging or awkward. However, Mill has his own theory of true moral
conscience, which he defines here as the force which
counterbalances impulse. A genuine conscience is personal. Authentic conscience is as individual as desire.
Both desire and restraint express my own vision of lire,
my own personal project, in postmodern terms.

○ '*Strong*' and '*weak*': Strength is a quality of the whole
person, a way of being. Mill argues that all the elements
of being are likely to expand together, or shrink in uni-
son. Repression is, therefore, never a way of making
'space' for growth. If you suppress one aspect of a person, you are lessening their whole scope for being. Like-
wise, weakness is a quality of the whole being of a person.

Mill thinks in terms of strong character and weak charac- 205
ter, rather than strong and weak characteristics. In this respect, his approach resembles that of the German nineteenth-century philosopher, Nietzsche.

**Implications**

Mill is proposing a theory of well-being as conflict. If socie- 206 ty attempts to regulate our desires from the outside, we will never experience this proper conflict, between *my* desire and *my* conscience. A society that represses desires will also destroy the possibility of conscience. In a world where nobody is allowed to experiment with impulse and desire, there will also be no experimentation with conscience and no new ethical life. New moral values grow alongside new desires. The moral inventors are likely to be those with rich inner lives, with fierce impulses. They will be the people who need to find a new balance.

207 More emotional does not mean less rational. People with stronger feelings will probably have richer reasons in response. Mill's theory of personality centres on wholeness of being.

---

**Mill and modern psychology**

Well-being means wholeness. The greater the wholeness, the greater the well-being. Our being grows through conflict.

---

208 Mill has been accused of having only a negative approach to liberty, but that accusation seems unfair in the context of his theory of well-being. Liberty is the condition most friendly to the widest possible well-being of humanity, and Mill has quite a full and rounded vision of that well-being. He is at least as concerned to create a new language for individuality as he is to deconstruct the claims of moralistic censorship and traditional authority. Mill is not merely anti-

authoritarian; he has an affirmative ideal of the human individual.

Mill has also been accused of failing to connect his liberal 209 theory with his utilitarian philosophy. Again, this seems unfair in the context of his arguments about individuality. He is a liberal because of his utilitarianism—in the sense that he sees liberty as the proper condition for the maximum promotion of the interests of humankind.

# Applied Liberty

210 In this chapter, we look at the way Mill draws his arguments together. In the later parts of *On Liberty*, he focuses on issues of his own day and on more specific recommendations and anti-recommendations. This more applied discussion runs from the end of Chapter Ⅲ ('Of Individuality') through Chapter Ⅳ ('Of the Limits of the Authority of Society over the Individual') and Chapter Ⅴ ('Applications'). Though the sections are lively and provocative, they do not change substantially the argument or introduce new concepts or terms.

211 Since Mill is now concerned with practical applications, it seems most appropriate to look at these parts in the context of specific cases from our own day. We can then ask whether the ideas still apply to particular cases. We have already seen that the general concepts are still very much

alive; but perhaps the more applied side of *On Liberty* has dated.

# THE ' FREEDOM TO BE YOURSELF' CAMPAIGN

On the BBC News for Wednesday, 10 January 2001, it was 212 announced that:

> *A jury has unanimously cleared a veteran nudist cam-paigner of being a public nuisance.*

The man was Vincent Bethell, founder and leader of the 213 Freedom to be Yourself Movement. To protest against the arbitrary requirement to be clothed in public, he had staged naked protests and had previously been found guilty by magistrates. This was his first jury trial and the ten men and two women had cleared him of the charge. In court, Bethell exclaimed: ' *Being human is not a crim.* ' He was warned by the judge not to count his legal chickens: ' *I wouldn' t go away too much with that idea. It is simply not a public nuisance in these circumstances.* '

Reporting the event next day, *The Guardian* newspaper in- 214 formed its readers that the defendant was ' *the first person to stand trial in an English court naketd*' .

The case clearly enters one area explored by *On Liberty*. Is 215 this an eccentric individual being prevented from express-ing his chosen identity? Or is he in fact harming others? In court, the prosecution claimed that his behaviour was bound' *to harm the morals of the public or their comfort, or to obstruct the public in the enjoyment of their rights*' . The Freedom Movement insisted ( *The Guardian*, 28 July 1999 ) that there was no harm to others in ' *non-sexual peaceful public nudity*' . In one incident, where Bethell perched na-ked on a lamppost, a passer-by was quoted as saying: ' *Onlookers were not shocked by the protest and the pro-testers were doing no harm.* '

216 There was a dark side to the story, as well as a lighter tou-ch. Prior to the trial, Bethell had been kept in solitary in Brixton prison for two months because, as a remand pris-oner, he refused to wear clothes:

> He said by telephone that he was locked naked in his 11ft by 7ft cell most of the day and night. . . He had no visitors, he said, being kept out of the visitors' centre for fear of offending inmates and visitors, and no out-side exercise, for fear he cut his feet.

*The Guardian*, 9 November 2000

217 How does Mill' s applied discussion relate to this case? In his chapter on applications Mill rather reluctantly adds a few remarks about decency, mainly pointing out that *On Liberty* is not concerned with the question of indecency but with the wider problem of individual self-expression. He does say that there are ' many acts' that are fine in private but not in public. His tone is you restrained. He calls such indecency ' *a violation of good manners* ' . He then de-

clares that as such it can be stopped. With an audible murmur of distaste or even embarrassment, Mill notes: ' *Of this kind are offences against decency; on which it is unnecessary to dwell.* '

Mill would clearly not be a member of the Freedom to Be  218 Yourself Movement. In fact, he might well see such a campaign as a dangerous travesty of liberal ideals. At the same time, if he did object to Bethell' s actions, it would be under the low-key heading of ' violation of good manners' , rather than in any terms like harm to public morals. Clearly, good manners belong to their time; they can change, and if so, then the limits of permissible action can change. It does seem unlikely you could justify keeping a person in solitary confinement for bad manners. So far we can see how Mill' s language still offers a more refined and humane tone than that in which moral controversy is currently conducted.

Other passages might at least make us hesitate before ap-  219 plying legal sanctions to such campaigners. Mill laments that' individuals are lost in the crowd' . He adds positively that:

---

**QUOTATION**

Precisely because the tyranny of opinion is such as to make eccentricity a reproach, it is desirable, in order to break through that tyranny, that people should be eccentric.

---

220  Does wearing no clothes count as a desirable eccentricity? One suspects, from the squeamish passage on public decency, that for Mill it may not! But he does give us a different question to ask. Instead of simply wondering whether these displays do no real harm, we can also ask whether this is possibly an admirable eccentricity, in a time of conformity whether this is just a misguided person who has confused independence with rudeness. *On Liberty* does not really give ready answers to such cases. The aim of the book, carried through in its more applied later stages, is to make us ask richer questions and use more refined terms.

221  The case of the naked campaigner is a classic illustration of the fact that Mill's question, from his Chapter IV' Of the Limits to the Authority of Society over the Individual', remains *our* question:

> **QUOTATION**
>
> What, then, is the rightful limit to the sovereignty of the individual over himself?

222  Mill's arguments encourage us to keep asking this question and not to substitute our unthinking reactions for this process of inquiry. It may be that the Freedom to Be Yourself campaigner has violated good manners to the point where we are entitled to stop him. On the other hand, maybe we should express our distaste in ways that fall short of actually restraining him.

Mill is not in favour of a'stiff upper lip'world where every- 223
one ignores everybody else and pretends that nothing un-
usual is happening. We might find humane ways to voice
our annoyance, if we decide that this person is not really
harming anyone, but is still failing to meet appropriate
standards:

> **QUOTATION**
>
> What I contend for is, that the inconvenciences which are
> strictly unseparable from the unfavourable judgement of oth-
> ers, are the only ones to which a person should ever be sub-
> jected for that portion of his conduct and character which
> concerns his own good, but which does not affect the interest
> of others in their relations with him.

Possibly, we should subject him to the'inconvenience'of 224
our disapproval. On the other hand, it could be that *we*
should suffer his behaviour as a necessary'inconvenience':

> **QUOTATION**
>
> But with regard to the merely contingent or, as it may be
> called, constructive injury which a person causes to society
> be conduct which neither violates any specific duty to the
> public, nor occasions perceptible hurt to any assignable indi-
> vidual except himself, the inconvenience is one which society
> can afford to bear, for the sake of the greater good of human
> freedom. If grown persons are to be punished for not taking
> proper care of themselves.

You might well feel that wearing no clothes is'not taking 225 proper care' of oneself. In fact, the prison authorities seem to have used this as a pretext for denying Bethell exercise rights: he might cut his feet in the yard. Mill's passage encourages us to wonder if the yard should not have been made safer for him! It also makes one sense a certain bad faith in such reasons.

226 Mill makes us realize how serious a thing it is to limit' the sovereignty of an individual'. Every time we feel we have to restrain someone like the Freedom to Be Yourself activist, we are deciding to lessen the sum of human freedom. It may be justifiable, if we really feel he is denying our access to a decent social environment, but we must always use the least possible intervention, and we must be honest about our motives. Are we sure it is his bad manners that are intolerable? Or are we just outraged by his non-conformity:

> **QUOTATION**
>
> There are many who consider as an injury to themselves any conduct which they have a distaste of, and resent it as an outrag to their feelings.

227 We may feel distaste, but is it really doing us any harm—or are we harming ourselves by the excessiveness of our own reactions and our inability to control our feelings of disgust? *On Liberty* retains an extraordinary power of refining and enriching the coarse terms in which we often express our reactions to other people's awkward behaviour.

# BOUND TO STAY SILENT? MILL AND THE WHISTLEBLOWER

On Tuesday, 16 March 1999, Europe awoke to a startling 228 announcement:

> Europe was left decapitated last night as the entire European Commission resigned en masse after a devastating report by an independent commission.
>
> The Guardian

The commission's President, Jacques Santer, came from an emotional commission meeting just after midnight.

BBC News

The news was bleakly grand. This was a world-scale 229 event, the disappearance of the entire ruling body of one of the great blocs. The BBC was excitedly grim:

> The European Union has been plunged into deep crisis following the resignation of all *20* Commissioners. . . it was still unclear how the EU would continue.

But all of this had begun with the actions of one minor Eu- 230 ropean Union official, a Dutch accountant named Paul van Buitenen. In early December 1998 this official wrote an internal report specifying widespread fraud and mismanagement. Fearing that it would be suppressed, he passed a copy of this report to the Green Party in the European Parliament. In response, he was suspended on half pay. It was noted in reports that when officials had been accused of corruption, they were suspended on full pay.

231 The Greens circulated the report, and on 17 December 1998 the EU Parliament tabled motion of no confdence in the Commission. After initial delays and denials, the President, Jacques Santer, admitted irregularities may have occurred.

232 An inquiry was established. Meanwhile, van Buitenen had been accused of ' imparting information to unauthorised and non-competent persons'. The BBC reported on 6 January 1999 that:

> The Commission says he was suspended for breaking his contract by releasing details of the inquiry.

233 An EU spokeswoman explained in justification that: ' *The report should have been kept secret while the case is under investigation*'. At the same time, the' whistleblower'. as he became known, faced other pressures. *The Guardian* noted( 11 January 1999)' *barely veiled allegations that he is mad*'. He was said to be a religious fanatic and a political extremist:

> I admit that part of my motivation is that I am a Christian. . . I did not realise that was an offence. Then they say I am an extreme right-winger. . . I am a member of the Green party.

*The Guardian*. 13 October 1999

Yet when the inquiry was reported, van Buitenen's claims 234 were endorsed, with spectacular results.

Mill did, in fact, consider the argument about people bind- 235 ing themselves to limit their own freedom of action and expression. Should the whistleblower have honoured the 'gagging' clause in his own contract, and kept his report secret until it had been considered by the requisite authorities? His acceptance of the original job contract was, in Mill's terms, a' mutual agreement' and:

> **QUOTATION**
>
> . . . it is fit, as a general rule, that those engagements should be kept. Yet, in the laws, probably, of every country, this general rule has some exceptions. . . engagements which violate the rights of third parties. . . injurious to themselves.

In other words, contracts should generally be honoured, 236 but there must be exceptions. People cannot be bound by agreements which deny them basic freedoms or which bind them to act against the real interests of others, or to harm themselves. The EU had argued that this dissident had been suspended for' breaking his contract', but Mill specifically insists, in reply, that a person cannot always be held to' *the fulfilment of the contract*'.

Freedom of expression, and of individuality, can sometimes 237 override the literal' fulfilment' of the terms of a contract. For example, following Mill, we could argue that the interests of the citizens of Europe would have been harmed if the information had *not* been revealed. We could also argue that van Buitenen's own interests required the disclosure: could he have withstood the counter-pressure on his own?

238 Several of Mill's arguments seem to come together around this famous case. The disclosure of the information is an example of free expression, which has turned out to serve the' permanent interests' of the wider world. From the hostile responses of the authorities, it seems reasonable to wonder if they would ever have acted on this report had it not been made public. Their counter-action, through the media, seems to have involved the attempt to stigmatize individuality as well as to suppress freedom of discussion. It seems that expression and individuality still go together. Those authorities that try to prevent expression seem also to be antagonised by difference, or even eccentricity.

239 Does the story have a happy ending? The whistleblower was reemployed, but apparently not given back his original job:

> He was reinstated by the commission... but was moved to an accounting unit dealing with the non-controversial ordering of furniture.

*The Guardian.* 13 October 1999

240 He wrote a book, which the authorities tried to prevent being published. Is this a further case of punishing individuality and restricting expression? The authority argued that there were good reasons, at least for suppressing the book:

The commission has no desire to suppress freedom of speech. but the civil rights of those who are the subject of allegations must be protected.

Was van Buitenen's book prejudicing the fair trial or assessment of those accused of corruption?If so, the censorship might be justified on grounds of' harm to others'. But is that the real motive?A court decided in favour of the whistleblower.                                                                241

Mill recognizes cases where harm to others is not a good enough reason for censorship:                                      242

---

**QUOTATION**

... it must by no means be supposed, because damage, or probability of damage, to the interests of others, can alone justify the interference of society, that therefore it always does justify such interference.

---

Even if van Buitenen's book damaged the interests of some others, that might still not be a good enough reason to prevent its publication. This is surely a case of' probability of damage' or even possibility of damage. But again that could be outweighed by the value to society of letting a neglected fragment of the truth be heard, even if it is expressed intemperately.                                            243

In his *Autobiography*, Mill warned that *On Liberty* was a book for the future. We remain citizens of Mill's future, and we still need his arguments.                                             244